A Wish for
Someone to Listen

A Wish for
Someone to Listen

—————————————————

Tiffany Hobbs

To order additional copies of this book, contact:
Xlibris
1-888-795-4274
www.Xlibris.com
Orders@Xlibris.com
698717

I WANNA DEDICATE THIS BOOK TO MY WONDERFUL CHILDREN, WHO HAS INSPIRED ME TO NEVER GIVE UP AND TO KEEP LIVING EVERYDAY. MOMMY LOVES YOU ALL MORE THEN LIFE IT'SELF, DEMETRIU' FULTON YOU ALWAYS SAID MOMMY YOU CAN DO IT, IM SO PROUD OF YOU. I LOVE YOU BIG GIRL, AND IV'E DONE THIS FOR YALL.

If you're reading my story then you will know the truth about my life, I'm not rich or famous but I am human with a story to tell. I'm a survivor and I've made it through my storm. God is still working on me as I am not yet perfect. I had to learn not to reflect on the negative things as I gotten older, in hopes of sorting it all out, and being smart as I was at seven years old wasn't an easy thing for adults to take in. I was tired of being called a smartass; I was tired of always being asked if I was getting smart just because I was intelligent enough to answer a direct question, or speak up when I over heard someone making fun of or talking badly about my mom. I'm over a relative's house and hear the saying why did my mother turn out the way she did, why does she continue to deal with bullshit men, and who told her to have all them bad ass kids. LOL so I would butt in and say she grown her decisions are made by poor choice in judgment but she would learn, I got my ass whooped that day and many others. But when my mom came to pick us up No one would dare to speak the truth, They were lien talking about it was a differant reason that I had gotten a whoopen a normal family conversation at my home was never about happy times or positive things, unless someone had something they were giving to buy one's friendship. It's not a secret that my mom was the black sheep of her family. Visiting certain relatives became uncomfortable because we knew they were talking about us, they giggled often about the clothes and shoes we wore. I overheard my aunt say my mom should be ashamed of her damn self. Now we wasn't rich but we were on what most people today call's a fixed income. Growing up back then I never understood why most times my mom would say we can't visit certain family members, some members of the family thought we were embarrassing them by the way we looked and dressed. But some of them were also undercover drug addicts, alcoholics. They just were looking to keep the attention off their self I will never turn my back on my children, I really thought I was a typical teenager growing up I too gotten into mischief like other children my age, I remember being in the seventh grade in the lunchroom, my stomach hurted so bad it started feeling like I was wet between the legs, so I placed my hand between and wiped a little bit I then brung my hand up so I only could see what it was, it was blood and oh my God I almost panicked so I quickly gotten up and tied my jacket around my waist and I went home, when I gotten home my mom was on the couch talking on the phone, she quickly said wut are you doing here so early. I think I started my period I explained, OH GOD she said to the person on the phone let me call you back, she called everybody and there daddy that day Tip started her period. She baked cupcakes with chocolate icing on them she went to the store and brung me a balloon and a small gift bag, I'm thinking to myself wow I should bleed more often, I opened the bag there were different maxi pads. I was confused because I was so embarrassed by the phone calls I thought that was nobody's business but ours. Now the funny thing is I was expecting this same treatment after the second period came hahahahahahhh there was no cake no balloon no nothing okay she bleeding was all. I also had my first taste of beer that day I stolen from my mom's cup when she went out the room, I thought it was plain old awful. I couldn't see how grown ups drank that stuff. My discovery of abuse began at eight months old, and not at seven years old as I grown up to know, I noticed these marks on my left thigh and I asked my mom were I had gotten them from. She told me that when I was eight months old she sat me on the ironing board to iron my stepfather's shirt for work. She said she turned away for a minute and when she came back that my leg was shaking and she had taken me to the hospital for treatment, I asked if they thought she had done this to me she said no they just treated me and sent us back home. I seriously had alot of doubt about that so I never said anything else in regards to the story, shortly after that my mom and stepfather argued and faught all the time. When they yelled it scared me, when they faught I also scared me. When my stepfather became angry his eyes bucked out of his head and his nostrils flared open really wide, He almost looked monsterous to me. And when he thought that I had done something bad he would say to me in a very angry voice, "get your little ass somewhere and sit down before I beat your ass. I would run over and try to get onto the couch but it was hard at a year old my lil legs couldnt reach, so he grabbed me by the arm and slung me on the couch, while yelling didn't I say get on the dam couch. Now my older sister was always in our room playing with the lil kitchen set my mom had gotten from the free church, so she rarely gotten in to trouble I was just trying to be under my mom all the time, but always at the wrong times. I was scared of him, he had my mom going out begging family and friends for money to support his drug habbit, by pretending the kids needed things . . . my sister knew when I had gotten a whooping or something she always would say in a three year old voice, "come on baby are you ok, our little room had a twin bed and a baby bed. I remember being stuck in that bed for hours, but my sister got up on the chair and always helped me get out, come on baby she would always say. We would play on the lil kitchen set, we had fake food and dishes to pretend cook, when we ate real food we had a little multicolored table and chairs to sit at. I had written on the wall once with crayons and my stepfather tore my legs up, he left all kinds of marks on me just for writing on the dam wall, when my mom came home she asked why was I crying he said she had wrote on that wall over there so I beat her ass. My mom was pissed off, she said look wut youhave done to her legs, you had no reason to hit my baby. My stepfather said fuck you and her, mom had started pulling out clothes to wash at the laundry mat, my stepfather got up got dressed and said ill be back. And he didnt come back until later that night so mom couldnt go to the laundry the mat because they wasnt twenty four hour's. The next day mom was getting ready to go to the laundry mat, and I didnt want to stay with my stepfather because he always found an excuse to beat us. So I ended up trying to go with mom anyway, she opened the door to the apartment and we emediatly started crying, my mom pulled they cart holding the two big bags of clothe's and another bag she pulled to the top of the stairs, I grabbed onto the cart as she was heading down stairs. My sister was looking over the railing, my step father wasn't watching us he had the door still open and was watching tv yelling yall get in here, too late mom never knew I was behind the cart until I started screaming, oh my God she screamed my stepfather leaped over the raililng, my baby done fell, now they thinking I had fallen over the rail but I was drug by the cart my face was a bloody mess I had knocked my two front teeth out, my mom had taken me to the hospital, and when we gotten back home mom still couldn't make it to the laundry mat, she sat me on the couch and removed my shoes, and coat she got some ice and placed it into the plastic pouch the hospital had given her to put on my mouth, and even though it was cold I didnt move my mouth was sore and I couldnt eat anything but soft foods, yogart, pudding, applesauce, and gelo. My sister gave me a hug and kissed me on my jaw she said are you ok baby, my stepfather burst out and said yeah she okay she shouldn't have taken her little ass out there in that hallway. Mom continued to leave us with this man, he knew my mouth was sore so he waited to physically abuse us, so he verbally abused us instead.

I knocked his cup of beer over and he back handed me in my mouth so hard that my head hit the wall he didnt even care to check and see if I was hurt he just continued to curse, after he gotten the mess up he grabbed me by one arm and took me to my room where he threw me onto the floor, yelling at the same time "sit your little ass down and dont move" I didnt know where my sister was at the time she didnt come in the room until he left out she was using the bathroom. She kept trying to pick me up off the floor but I was scared that our stepfather would come back in the room I just laid there a cried. My sister just held my head in her lap she kept saying it's ok baby ima tell momma, my stepfather must have listening the whole time cause he yelled, 'tell yo momma, my sister jumped as he continued the bitch need to teach yall some dam manners, so yall can stop fucking with shit. He opened the door and said if you tell yo momma anything im'a whoop your ass too! and mom came soon after she asked us why were we crying and why was we on the floor all we could do was point at our stepfather. She quickly asked him what was going on and why were we crying so hard, he said they need to learn how to stop fucking with shit. Wut did they do now mom asked him, Tip knocked over my dam beer and they keep fucking with shit and im tired of it. Mom argued with him for a while then he left for the day but mom got us dressed and washed our hands and faces she walked us down the street to the park, stopping at the store first, we got some juices and chips, I dont remember him feeding us when ever my mom left but she made sure to do so whenever she got back home. But we went on to the park and played for a couple hours, till it was time to go. Mom bathed us and fed us and put us some comfortable clothing. My stepfather finally decided he would come back, he was drunk and staggering, "shugga" fix me something to eat im hungary too! So mom fixed something to eat as well she took it to him in the bedroom they shared together, he was always angry when he drank. So once he finished his food we were still eating and he said put them to bed im sleepy, mom said once I finish my food ill put them down. And hurry up he said, so once we were done mom took us to our room she tucked us in and went in her room. The next morning we thought we were about to watch cartoons but dad had already turned the channel to some western movie he wasnt even watching it cause he was to busy watching us waiting for us to do something wrong . . . he got up without eating breakfast he was late for work, he quickly gotten dressed and left he never came back right after work he had to stop and get drunk wherever it was that he would go. When he came back he was so drunk he had urinated on himself, he banged on that door so loudly that he disturbed the neighbors, they were yelling back and forth, mom was laying on the couch and me and my sister was laying on her we were watching a movie mom was asleep. Dad banged and cursed, mom finally got up to answer the door, he was just now removing his keys from his pocket, when mom said why are you being so rude and the kids in here you know your being to loud. Shut the fuck up he said, and rushed pass her sitting on my foot as he removed it from underneath himself. He yelled yall go to bed and let me lay here, so we got up and went in our rooms. The next morning he was sitting on the couch smoking a cigarette, mom and he was talking about seperating for a while my stepfather packed his belongings and left he and my mom didnt get back together for about two years . . . my sister was almost four years old but still three she invited him over for dinner, she had to run to the store so he watched us until she got back but before she left my sister tried to follow her out when my stepfather had tried to grab her by the shirt he accidently scratched her on the face, during this same month I wasn't aware that my grandmother was watching my mother because of the scratch she started suspecting abuse of some kind and because I was still to young to explain she was removed from the home and I was left there, my grandmother said she wasn't going to put up with nobody neglecting her granddaughter. I missed my sister a lot she was all I had, that was my protection, my sister ended up staying with her father and his mother. My family told her so many lies about how she was taken out the home and that it was all my mom's fault. I still carry that hurt today, how could they show favor and remove my sister and not me I was getting the worse abuse and they continued arguing and fighting after my sister left. Although my mom has been labeled the black sheep of the family it hurts to see most of her brothers and sisters and only a selected few will speak. My mom had something happen to her growing up as well as to where her mother's boyfriend took her on a job site and raped her that's how my sister ended up being conceived. My grandmother didn't want my mom to keep the baby because of the incident so she tried to get her an abortion, which was a bad decision someone realized so my sister is her today. That made it hard for the immediate family to except us in there home's instead of us being placed in foster home. And the foster home is where we ended up.

It's sad because living in my thirty's today, me and that side of the family was never close I felt as if they didn't like me and that hurt me so much. The only time we were able to come together was for a funeral service, it has gotten so bad that we don't even attend the family reunion's anymore. I used to be sad about things, but not anymore the truth is family can sometimes be your worst enemies, and your friends sometimes treat you better. Blood is supposed to be thicker than water, I have learned that blood can also be diluted and thinned out. It's a shame that children have to get involved in grown up business. Even though family issues come up, a family is supposed to be there for one another and stick together, in my family that wasn't the case and I honestly feel that children wasn't supposed to repeat wut the hear, or wut was going on inside the home you lived in. Or there would be a consequence, as I started feeling unhappy and unloved by many. How do you work out the fairness between siblings and each one's own feelings, everyone needs their own space and room to grow. Everybody has a different personality, but when you notice things like why wasn't I given a gift on Christmas at family member's houses but the other kids did. How can you explain to a child why there wasn't enough? Being the oldest after my sister was taken away was very rough I had so much responsibility. I tried to do a good job keeping up with my younger siblings; I washed blue jeans at seven years old in the tub on my hands. Watching my mom being abused was very hard for me, I tried to call 911 emergency one time her and my stepfather had got into it. And why did I do that knowing she was already mad as hell, she didnt even go to court to prosecute, after the police left she cursed me out and told me that I shouldn't have called the police and that I needed to stay in a child's place, as painful as it was. I learned to just keep my mouth closed unless it was about my younger siblings, or myself. I remember being mommys little helper back when she was alot nicer, she used to let me help her make the cakes, she even saved me some of the batter so I can fix a small cake in my easy bake oven. And on father's day she used to let me make a cake for my dad, he was os happy once upon a time, he always gave me the first bite to make sure I aint poison it. When he went to the store later that day he always would bring me back this big bag of candy and say share with your brothers and sister's, my baby brother was a sugar head, we would go in our room and eat candy and play. We were bouncing off the walls, mom would come and tell us to quiet down so we wouldn't get into trouble. Sometimes it was extremely loud when mom and my stepfather had company over, most times they even faught while the company was there and some days they would wait until the company left. I felt sorry for my mom, but she told me to stay out of it and that she could handle herself, so I did. I remember when my mom and my stepfather first got together she used to get so pretty and go out and meet him, he used to be well dressed and well groomed. He drove a nice dark car, in the begining we only knew of the alcohol abuse and the marijuna they smoked, I later learned that my stepfather has gotten my mom started on drugs, at this point my mother has 5 children two of which was seamed to belong to my stepfather, he decides he wants to take us to meet his sister and her children, they were all about the same ages as us. But from that moment of introduction we all had gotten along so well, cousins we were. We gotten along very well, we soon started spending the nights at there house and they would also stay at our house. How ever one of her son's was a little older then all of us, so he became a big brother figure to us while we played outside, and if the grown up's needed to step out for a moment or two. He was goofy but he loved us as if we had known each other for years, he took up for us when other kids were being cruel, we used to play tag and hide and seek and freeze tag. Double dutch was our favorite he couldn't jump like us so he jumped straight up and down, lol we had some good time's together. We enjoyed going over there house to visit it was freedom away from home. When it was a school day we would cry to stay and they did the same, we would say ask yall momma can yall stay or they would say the same. When we was down there for visits we played with there friends because they lived next door, those were the kids that kept all the snacks.

And they didn't mind bringing snacks outside they shared with everybody, On the first of the month my cousins mom gave them money so my mom tried to give us money too, mom used to go to there house to wash our clothes, so that was extra time to visit . . . my aunt would take multiple pictures of us when we did visit. when my baby brother was born around the same time as her youngest son, her and my mom would dress the two alike. my aunt told my mom one day that her father would be visiting soon and that he had hoped to meet us. She said the next visit would be around thankgiving, and Christmas, my mom had agreed to meet him on thanksgiving . . . when we finally met the man he said hey yall im yah grandaddy, he hugged my mom then he hugged us realy tight, we weren't used to this sort of greeting. he was a very nice man, and well dressed he drove a nice car as well. He also pulled out his camara's and taken a thousand pictures we start acting silly with each other, we put bunny ears behind each other's head. we pushed each other down trying to be in the front of every picture, The way my aunt had opened up her home to us and the way her father loved us was the greatest feeling ever. it was freedom away from home. My aunts baby's father was around to he sort of kept his distance, when my stepfather was around they were best friends they drank together and talk shit to each other like grown up do. There was something about him that wasnt right to me and I couldn't figure it out right away . . . we went to visit an older aunt on my step father's side very often, she would cook a big dinner and we would eat then we would play until it was time to go back home, now this aunt was very mean, she yelled at us all the time even when we weren't doing anything bad. She couldn't stand me, because I wasnt my stepfather's real child so she made sure I knew she didnt like me. Mom made us stay at her house on the days she knew she wouldn't be home or she would leave a note on the door saying for us to go there. Now mom wouldn't come back sometimes till late, my aunt would say gone in the kitchen and fix a lunchmeat sandwhich until yall momma gets back. When mom finally came I would hear my aunt yelling at mom about paying her for being late picking us up. She also said now wut if wasn't here where would them kids have went, mom said im sorry ill pay you. On our way to our apartment, there was a strange man you will read about that stayed in the same building and on the same floor as us, he was always learking the hallway, I always thought this man was a lil strange. As we walked up the stairs towards the man he barely moved out the way. my mom said excuse us as she let us walk pass her to get pass him, Locking the door behind her, we heard him slam his door like he was mad about something, My mom said that mutha fucker must be crazy or out his dam mind. then she asked me to go in the kitchen and wash them dishes so she can cook before we came home from school. The next day after school let out I gathered up my younger siblings and proceeded to walk home, when we reached the street that was before our's I seen the strange man sitting there on the corner, I told my siblings to hold me hand so we went the back way that was like a short cut to the building so we wouldn't have to walk pass this man. But as soon as we got in the building the man was coming in the building at the same time we were, "yall want some candy he said" "No thanks I said, as I repeated to myself, please let my momma be home. she must have heard the kids being loud cause she slung open the door, "get in here she said. I quickly pushed them inside then I hugged her so tightly, im so glad to see you, she said yall go wash yall hands. mom has fixed fried chicken, pinto beans, and sweet corn bread. she even had juice and milk in the refridgerator, and when I looked up there was cearl and other stuff, for some reason mom didnt have company that day. She even played with us. the next morning mom was warming up the food from the day before she was washing clothes, and ironing, She had even cleaned up while we were sleeping, our room was spotless everything was put away. she combed our hair and put us on clean clothes. "Mom what's going on."I asked, Somebody called 241-kids on me Thursday and they came out while we was gone and they said they coming back today, My aunt had called them because she was upset that nobody paid her yet for watching us while my mom was out. She told them that mom didnt feed us and our house was nasty. So when the lady came out she said there was nothing wrong here im sorry I had to come out. My mom was so mad but she needed for the aunt to continue watching us so she paid her and bought her cigarettes and beer, it wasn't so bad going over this aunts house when other children was there, she would make us play in the hallway of the building or the entrance way. we attended Washington Park Elementary. School, and became aquanted with some other children on our street so we would all walk to school together. We were able to spend the night with the friends we walked with being because they lived in the building next to our's So we would stay over there instead of alway's going to the aunt's house all the time. We had started calling those kids our cousins, and were still cousins today . . . people say Home is where the heart is, Then why is it that when I was growing up thats where the hurt was at. No matter what was going on in my life I would alawys end up at home, I remember waking up out of my sleep from being so hungary, to get a drink of water. It had to be around 12;20pm my mom and stepfather had company of another man and women friend, they were sitting at the kitchen table there were plates, playing cards and candels burning. I seen a big bowl of ice and pot scrather's, my stepfather had a pipe in his mouth lighting the end of it blowing smoke mom was yelling get out go back in your room, I cried because all I wanted was some water. so when morning came I asked my mom why couldnt I get a drink of water she said mind yo buisness if you was sleep you wouldnt need no dam water . . . well later that night me and my siblings went to sleep early cause mom and my dad was having company, I had awaken out my sleep to my stepfather with his hands inside my paints, I jumped up he put his hand up to his mouth and said shhh! you bet not make a sound he removed his hand I noticed he was putting his penis back inside his paints, I still cant remember to this day what he was doing other then touching me. when morning came I tried to tell my mom what had happened, but all she kept saying was girl he aint thinking about you and from that day on I tried to keep my brother and sister away from him, Although he was there father he was a father figure for me and if he would touch me and hurt my feelings anybody could, I started to feel everyone was bad. Because some people are so cruel towards children they tend not to care wut they do to hurt you, I was being abused at a young age and nobody seemed to listen when I tried telling. but my stepfathers sisters, babydaddy had hurt me also when and during the time we lived in florida, it's scarey to say that I used to urinate on myself from being afraid to get up and go to the restroom because some one had touched me and made me feel uncomfortable. when I would go to the restroom it didnt have a lock on the door so I would have my back against the door holding it so I could change my underwear after washing up. My uncle used to try and peek in the bathroom or bedroom whenever i was getting dressed, "Hopping to the door with only one paint's leg in, He would be walking away saying, "Shhhh you better not say shit". Once I was done dressing and came out to be amungst the other children, He would be waiting patiently. But always staren or cutting his eyes at me. I was afraid of him, and I was so uncomfortable. His dimeanor about himself was arrogant and cocky he walked around with his chest stuck out, and he was short and ugly. but very mean and hateful towards his woman, he mistreated her even if he wasnt drinking and this was almost his sport. I could never understand how can one you love hurt you so bad. I have witnessed him picking her up and throwing her, I have also seen him backhand her in the mouth just like on the movies where she was knocked of her feet.

"My Story Begins Here"

Recognizing abuse you may not see it in the begining, but a child knows when something is not right . . . inside a home with abuse it can be a very scarey thing if someone has threatend you by saying if you tell there going to hurt you, when I was seven years old we moved on this boxed in street called wade st, It was a cross connection between liberty and elm streets, my attacker lived only two door's away from me, in the same building on the same floor this strange man was tall and very skinny he had slightly grey and black colored hair, dark complexion and he had woren glasses, He was always smoking . . . this particular man just stuck out from other's he was very creepy, he used to watch us from his window as we played outside and everytime I looked up he would jump back. after w were done playing, we would enter the hallway and he would be pretending he Just got home, He would be locking and unlocking his door, But I just seen him in the window. I'll tell my mom the man next door always watching us, my mom always said that dam man dont want you. And the man ended up almost ruining my life. Early one morning I don't remember if there was any school I cant remember the exact day it was but I remember mom got us all dressed to go over my aunts house where we were supposed to stay until she ran her snuck out to get high, or appointments that children couldn't attend far as buisness, but this day in particular she needed to go pick up her food stamps and do a lil groccery shopping. we left out and walked not far but around the corner and across the street to my aunts house, mom asked her if we could stay there until she went to the food office and do a lil shopping. my aunt said yes they can sit here can you please bring me some cigarette and a beer, mom said she left us. me and my brother and sister stood to the side while my aunt locked the door. follow me she said as as she led us into her huge bedroom, There was two large reclining chairs and a very large bed. Three of our cousin's was already sitting on the floor, we were so excited to see each other. Sit down as she pointed to the floor amung the kids was one of my favorite boy cousins, we had done everything together. we gotten our butts whooped at the same time we started lil small fires in the back yard and we shared snacks and went on our lil missions to mess with the older kids. we stolen things together, this was my right hand man, My aunt knew it to she looked at us with this mean face and pulled out this big black leather belt that she had cut into two, she splited the belt up the middle so it made two belts but it was still connected at the end, she held it up and said one make the blister and one makes the buster and yall going to feel it if yall move . . . So we just sat there whispering amungst each other laughing and snickering, we were plotting on who we was about to mess with. she held up that belt and said didn't I say be quiet. "yes mam" we said. she scared us becaus she had gotten up from her seat so fast we jumped back in the position we were sitting, throwing the belt on the bed as she left out to answer the the door, One of our uncles was bringing her some fruits and other foods. "Hey yall" he said. "hi" we all yelled, we giggled after she then came back in the room saying "tip" which was my nick name, go see if your mother already left tell her dont forget my cigaretts. "ok I said, I unlocked the door and went out the building, I ran across the street not paying attention to the cars that were passing, I walked into my building I was almost afraid to enter the building it was darker then usual and it also creacked. so I started jumping up the stairs singing this lil song we used for playing jumprope outside, 1+1=2, 2+2=4, 4+4=8, 8+8=16 finally at the top of the stairs I had to look back down, eighteen stairs! knocking on my door I heard the strange man had opened his door and peeked out, my moma as I knocked again even harder. momma I yelled again because the strange man had scared me, mom had already gone so as I walked away from the door as soon as I had gotten by the mans door he quickly opened the door and grabbed my arm covering my mouth with his other arm. I finally got your little ass he said, he threw me in his apartment and closed and locked the door I was crying and shaking, he threw me down on this queen sized bed that he had drug from the bedroom into the livingroom floor. I seen the kitchen and through the kitchen he had sheets hung at the doorways so I couldnt see in, he had the water running in the kitchen sink he was cursing the whole time, while he placed a knife to my neck and said that if I aint shut up he would kill me. I tried to stop crying but I just couldnt so I started sniffing something terrible, I remember wearing a red white and blue sailor dress, he reached under the dress and pulled down my painties until one leg was free, I was trying to hold my legs closed while he struggled with the knife by my neck he pushed my legs open then he placed his head down there for a whole ten minutes he was given me oral sex and asking me if I liked it, I was crying so hard all I could say was please jesus dont let this man hurt me, when I didn't answer him he pulled me up and started to unzip his paints he was moving so fast he seamed scared he pulled out his penis, I was shaking so bad I almost fell backwards again, I aint know wut to do. I was so afraid when he told me it was my turn and that I had to suck his dick. I couldnt believe this was happening to me so I yelled my sister is outside waiting on me in the rain and if I dont come back she going to get my daddy. "Dam" why didnt you tell me this, the man started shaking and putting his penis back in his paints he told me to pull my clothes up and he opened the door, he said if you dont come back ima come looking for you ima kill you if you tell. "Okay I said, I ran down the stairs missing about five I hurt my ankle but I made it back across the street crying and bangging on my aunts door let me in let me in, she opened the door asking me where the hell I been. I ran to the room facing the front street I saw the man looking for me he was scratching his head, and walking really fast. Oh my God he was looking for me, I was shaking and crying my aunt just kept on asking me where I been I never said a word. an half hour later my mom and stepfather came. my aunt said something is wrong with Tip, "Where is she my mom asked. momma came rushing in the room where I was sitting and she stood in front of me and kneeled down, I hugged her by the neck looking her in her eyes and telling her everything that happen even the part when I looked out the window and he was trying to find me. she started crying to my stepfather done left out the house my mom was calling the police, they told her to meet them at our building so we went on across the street I was still shaking, my stepfather was no where to be seen mom pulled me as she was walking fast, come on she said. I looked at the man's window moma daddy up there I said, as I pointed my daddy was kicking out the man window yelling come out of there with yo punk ass, my mom was yelling get down, My daddy done already went inside the man's apartment. you can hear them yelling from the second floor to the street the police had pulled up and jumped out there cars my daddy had the man trying to drag him onto the fire excape, freeze the police were yelling my daddy was beating the hell out of the man while the police where entering the hallway some had climbed the fire excape yelling freeze. they made them go out through the door where two officers met them and escorted them down to the street in hand cuffs my mom explained what had happened and that she was the one called the police, they let my dad go and kept the man they took us to the station where we had make a report and file charges againt the man. A couple weeks later we received a letter in the mail from the clerk of courts. we had to go down and meet with a couple of people. my lawyer and an officer along with the prosecutor had taken me into this room and asked me all kind of questions, they gave me a small cup full of sweet tarts and told me they were truth pills, I said that I didn't need no truth pills, they all started to laugh one man said there going to helpd you tell the truth they pulled out these two dolls one was a male the other was a female they had asked me if I could show them using these dolls wut the man had done to me. so I showed them everthing, the next visit was the exact same except this time they showed me where the bad man would sit in the court room and where I would sit, they said there was nothing to be afraid of and that I could sit there and practice if I wanted to, so I sat there. they told my mom that I was telling the truth and that everytime they asked wut happen I gave the same story word for word the man was sentenced to ten years in prison, I even met the judge afterwards he took me and my mother in his chambers he said im so sorry about wut had happen to you. He shook my hand and handed me a check for three thousand dollars and told my mom to buy me whatever I wanted . . . my lawyer even told my mom she didnt have to pay him because I was a good sport. the next couple weeks was horrible because I still was afraid to come in and out of our apartment building, I used to have to go to the store for a couple people on my street, and one was an older man he seemed to be in his sixties, he was married and drove a nice car. Now this man was interested in young girls and everytime his wife wasnt around he didnt mind showing how much money he had, he showed off every chance he got. well one day my mom said mr thomas want you to go to the store for him. ok so I went over and knocked on the door he said come in I said no thanks ill wait here, he came out and said I need you to play these numbers for me and grabb a couple cans of pop. ok so he gave me the money and I went to the store and came back, he was sitting outside on the same corner the other guy sat on all the time. Mr thomas said thank you and took his bag he grabbed my arm handing me seven dollars, and spinning me between his legs I could feel myself bing pressed against his private part, so I got free and went back to the store and bought snacks for my younger siblings, I went in the house. the next day I came out and mr thomas said hey you do you wanna go to the store for me, no my mom said not today I said back to him, later he saw my mom and asked her why couldnt I go to th store for him my mom didnt know that I said I aint wanna got to the store for mr thomas she didnt even know wut he had done to me. so everytime he asked me to go to the store I said no. Some of the children in the neighborhood would make fun of us and call our mom a crack head or say things like yall momma smoke crack. and I would defend her by saying so wut and yo momma smoked with here and they would stop saying things to us. my stepfather's dad was coming to town to visit and he wantd to stop by our house to see us because my mom and aunt on my dad side wasnt seeing each other as much as before so he came to the house and brung all these pictures we had taken during his last visit. He brung us a bike and brung my baby brother a big wheel, he gave my mom and dad money for there gifts. we felt so special because I wasnt even his natural granddaughter and he made me feel as if I were he never showed any favor between us, even today it a tradition that he would come up every christmas and take us shopping for our kids he would give us five or six hundred dollars each, me my sister and two other girl cousins he would make sure that we tell our no good baby daddy's that grandaddy bought this. lol we love our granddaddy, my baby brother was a year old almost two years old but he talk real good, I loved him so much I treated him as if he was my own son . . . when he would get into trouble he would run to me and my mom didnt like that she would always say thats not your momma. so everytime he did something I would take the blame if he got a spankin I used to get teary eyed and ask mom to stop spankin him. he used to mess with everything, I remember he asked my mom for some milk and she had told him no, he came looking sad I asked wut was wrong he said I want some milk, so I went and poured him some and told him to hurry up and drink it. and he would hurry up and drink it. I had to wipe his mouth everytime beacuse he had a milk mustache, he cried when I had to leave out the house for a while, but mom wouldn't let me take him with me so I would sneak him out whenever I knew she was good and high. I was seven years old when I first started going to the store by myself, I knew how to change pampers, wash the dishes, I used to wash our clothes out on my hands for school just so we would have things clean. I had done everything for my baby brother that a mother would do except breast fed him, lol. now he is three years old and im ten he would have accidents on himself if he urinate he would stand ther and scratch his shoulders and if he booboo he would pick his eye lashes I would hurry up and change him so mom wouldn;t know because he got a whoopen for it . . . my stepfather had a job selling these big pictures you hang on the wall, so he started taking me and my sister with him to help him sell them and he would give us five dollars one time he let us pick a small picture and I picked out this tupac picture, my sister picked out another kind of picture. the next week we learned that my stepfather had other children from cheating on my mom, so he had gotten us all together and bought us some outfits alike and took us to this well known movie theater for easter they were striped dresses with the matching lil purse's, they were all differant colors I think mine was tourqoise and my sisters was pink, the other girls had on yellow and purple, we were pretty and I was still trying to figure out where did these kids come from. I didnt know where my dad sudden case of the niceness came from but I was happy with it he bought popcorn and hotdogs and boxs of candy from the theater, so we enjoyed ourselve's at the show that day. but im so nosey I realized everytime these girls came around he was nice so we need them to come to our house to visit more often. even though it didnt last that long. my mom and dad's drug problem was getting worse the car had gotten tooken the furniture inside the house started disapearing, one day we came home from school the neighbor stopped us in the hallway and said yall mom is not home but yall can sit here till she comes back so while sitting there I noticed that the fish tank this person had was just like our's hey where did you get this fishtank from I asked "oh yo momma sold it to me" we just got very quiet I saw my picture on the wall when mom came home true enough our fish tank was missing and my picture was too, there was some food missing out the freezer. if we ask questions my mom would say none of yall dam buisness, we will get it back and we never did, everytime she was upset that she couldnt get high she would make us clean the house, she told us to go in our room and start taking them dam clothes out th closet. we was standing on the bed when she got in the room, wut yall doing up ther she asked we just saw a mouse run in the closet. Yall aint seen shit get down she said, so we was sitting on the bed and she was just digging away then she yelled there it go she couldnt get up fast enough so she hit her head on the wall and fell back down her legs were in the air me and my sister was cracking up laughing, my momma was pissed "she said" yall laugh at any dam thing and when she thought it was safe to dig again she did. Finally the clothes was off the floor and put away nicely in the closet me and my sister still laugh to this day and my mom still gets mad. growing up in Cincinnati downtown over the rhine area, was sweet we knew everybody and everybody knew us I used to go the bar where my real dad was supposed to be he was in this bar fun sun up to sun down, he would sit me on them high bar stools. The owner knew I was my fathers child so he never would ask me to leave even though children wasn't allowed in the bar, I felt special. my dad would sit and pick all my nail polish of my fingernails he would say your to pretty to wear make up and polish he said never wear make up, I asked why he said you will ruin my face, I said daddy how my wearing make up will ruin yo face, he said cause your face is my face. his breath always smelled of Windsor Canadian which was his favorite drink. he would walk to that old juke box and play Al-Green's love and happiness, which by the way is my favorite song. my dad used to tell me that he was going to buy me some shoes them l.a gears with the differant colored shoe strings, he told me this for three years them shoes done went out of style, but I loved hearing him talk, then he would gave me my li fifteen dollars and walk me out the bar, I would stop at the candy store on my way home an get the other kids everything they liked.

my lil brother knew when I had something because he would be jumping up and down, and when I gave him all that he wanted he would have a jaw full of stuff. sitting on the edge of the bed his feet would be rocking real fast backwards then forwards, my mom and stepfather had started back hanging at his sisters house so they were almost always gone. So I would have to warm up the food in a microwave if she cooked anything or fix what ever was quick in the microwave so we wouldnt be hungary. ill make sure or clothes was together and ready for the school day. we stayed in the same room because I was afraid of wut may happen when it gets dark, my baby brother stayed right next to me at all times my sister was on my opposite side and my other brother was at the foot of us. I used to be so tired in the mornings because I tried to stay awake so no one would hurt them while they slept, I had even start pushing our dresser to the door so I would be able to hear wut was going on. then I thought about bringing a bucket in the room incase we had to use the bathroom nobody had to leave the room. the next day my mom asked what are yall doing in there and wuts on this door, she said move it or get an ass woopen, my stepfather had started back beating my mom. she used to let him talk all kinds of shit to her and she never said nothing back. I used to take my siblings outside so they wouldn't have to worry about what was going on in the next room when the grown up's was inside smoking and drinking. because I had taken up for the kids all the time I had gotten a whoopen because my little brother not the baby had threw a rock at somebodys window, and when we went in the house we tried to go straight in our bedroom without telling mom the window was broken so mom went to the store and we didnt even know she had left out the house so the neighbors told her that my brother had broken this window, but I had spoken up and said he didnt do it I did but I didnt meen to hit the window I tried to hit a bird, but she didnt care wut I tried to hit she was mad them people window was broken, So I got a whoopen. my brothers and sister would run to me and ask if I was okay I would say yes are yall okay there heads would node really fast yeah they would say softly as if they were afraid to speak. we were always afraid to ask momma anything after she was mad. She would be mad the whole day. I remember I had got suspended from school because I didnt want to get a swat for continuing to chew gum during class so my teacher made me pick one he said get suspended or get suspended I had gotten enough whoopen's at home so I chose to be suspended I had an aunt that stayed down the street from the school so I had to call my mom and let her know that I had gotten suspended from school and that I was on my way home she said dont come her till after school was out. so I went to my aunts house it was friday and I couldnt return to school until wenesday and my mom had to bring me back. When

I had gotten home my mom was waiting she tore me butt up, when wenesday finally came she forgot she had to take me to school so I went to my aunts house and she took me to school now this was my favorite aunt she was young but ten years older then me. she will always hold a special place in my heart, I used to play sick at school and had to leave early so I could go over my aunts house. my mom always said dont come home till school was out so I used to go to my aunts house until after school. my aunt always needed me to she wanted me to go to the store for her, I would help her clean up her house feed her kids and take out the trash, I was at her house so much people thought I was her daughter. one day I was visiting and her boyfriend stopped by to show her his new bb gun, he started shooting us with it. I ran in the bathroom and locked the door behind me he chased my aunt in her room, he got on his knees and started shooting under the bathroom door he shot me in the foot my shoe had a bb in it we were yelling screaming for him to quit. the bathroom window was open and I could see the building entrance so when he finally left I ran out and locked the door. I told my aunt he was gone, she came out the room ducking cause she thought he was still inside the house. we laughed and she didnt let him back in so after school I walked home I ran out her complex so he wouldnt see me leave. thats wut I got I should have stayed in school that made me go to school everyday. I remember my mom telling me she was going to give a birthday party at ten years old so I told two kids from school and the kids on my street that that I talked to, February 22 came it was a thursday after school I was so excited to see wut I had gotten for my birthday that I got my younger siblings and we were rushing home when I got ther it didnt look like a party to me my mom di make a cake it was leaning a little bit but I aint care it was cake, I aint see no baloons but she was fixing Hot Dog's that she had just gotten from the free church the also gave her two bags of cookies that goes on the ice cream sandwhiches she had them laying out she had chips and bread. I looked in the fridge there was juice and icecream in the freezer now I aint see no paper plates or cups, one of my friends I call my cousins had ran home and got some cups because her dad brung them from work all the time. we borrowed the Neighbor's small boom box and plugged it up in the hallway were we all were mom had bread for the hot dogs but no ketchup my friend also went and got the ketchup and some mustard, so we were cool until it was time to eat the cake and ice cream, my momma said she forgot the paper plates so she tore up some brown paper bags and served the cake on it, when I tell yall these kids laughed at me the next day at school. I was so embaressed. they called my party a crack head party . . . lol . . . I never wanted another party after that and I never gotten another party af⁺er that, if my mom brung up party I laughed and said no thanks. my younger brother and sisters were happy doe because They ate cake and Ice cream on our real plates they didnt care "Thank's mom", my mom always talked about she wanted to move and change her life for the better, my stepfathers sisters o man used to beat her so bad everyday that her discission to leave wasnt the best thing she could have done my aunt and mom had gotten so close that they told each other everything she told my mom one day that she was moving to Daytona Beach Florida she said she couldnt take it any more and she was tired of doing drugs and that she was tired of supplying her mans drug habbit. she told my mom that she promised to write and call and that she would even send for us once she had gotten settled. they mom and aunt had embraced and cried they hugged and that was that, she said she would leave next week when her man went to work, she had saved some money and she had a relative that lived down there and they was waiting for her. so we went home and after school they day my aunt left my mom was crying and we asked her wut was wrong she said aunt louis had went to florida to live and we were sad to. The next month my mom got that call that she can come on down my aunt had sent for us, so my mom switched her mail to the address in florida where we would staying and when my step father went to work we were gone. she had the electric and everything cut off. mom forgotten to call my aunt first and tell her not to write because we were on our way so she wouldnt write. when we finally arrived in Daytona we called my aunt to let her know we was there she was so excited because she didnt rally think we was coming. waiting at the location given my uncle met us at the stop in a big fancy truck he lived right behind my aunt so he took us to her house. it was a large apartment complex there were townhome's it was beautiful it had this large fountain in the front yard, and my aunt and her kids were waiting outside to greet us as we pulled im we were so excited to see them as well my mom and my aunt hugged and cried on each other for so long. mom said she miss home already my aunt said look how far you have come you can do it you will be fine. we went inside the only been ther two months and had a house full of furniture she gave us one of her son's room. to share until mom found a place. I loved picking the fruit from the trees, beacuse playing outside you didnt have to rush back in the house when you wer hungary, pears were my favorite. my mom used to pick lemons from the tree and make homemade lemonaide. we were in florida for about a month when my aunts problem had paid her a visit, her kids father was at the door, she looked like she seen a ghost. when she asked how did he find her he said a letter from shugga mailbox, shugga being my mom. aint that bout a bitch she said well you know im done with you I will call the police if you dont leave, she said as he started crying he said im sorry baby I changed I was lost without you . . . He was apologetic so she felt sorry and let him in, we never shared the room with my mom that was given to us we were in the room with the other kids and mom had that room all to himself. my aunts old man had pretended to have changed and two weeks later he was drinkin and acting stupid again. I was terrified when I seen him because of all the shit he done to me and the things I witnessed him do to her. he started to get upset because things weren't going his way. my aunt asked him over and over to not tell bob her brother that my mom had moved down to Daytona with the kids, and he agreed. my aunt wanted him to get a job so he could help out since he would be staying there and he wasnt feeling that he started drinking heavy. as for us as we would soon learn freedom was over . . . my uncle had gotten mad at my mom because my mom wouldnt give him money to support his habbit, so he cursed out my mom and my aunt because they wouldnt participate in his drug use, my aunt said that she wasnt going to allow that into her home any more. he walked out and slammed the door, my aunt was furious and my mother was also upset. my aunt cried to my mom about being scared of wut he would do now that her know where they were, later my mom and aunt went to work at a lil conveient store. my uncle aint been back for about five days he had a job last I heard in Cincinnati, so my aunt decided to call to see if he was ok, when he answered the phone she asked him where he was at and he said he was in cincinnati, with bob my stepfather my aunt asked him if he told Bob where Shugga and the kids was at. he said hell yeah I did and he wanna speak to Shugga, my aunt said you son of a bitch. He laughed, My aunt passed my mother the phone, when she realized whom she was speaking with she quickly hung up the phone, and four days later guess who was at the door, yes my stepfather and uncle, when my mom told us that he might have been coming down we wer scared. I was fearful being in the same house with both my uncle and my stepfather, being in florida was no differant from being in cincinnati at that time my aunt let them in because my stepfather was her brother the other was her babys father. the drugs and the drinking had gotten worse, my stepfather had a compulsive lien problem when he needed to get what he wanted. he had stolen peoples property for money he was stealing money from any body that he knew had any. he has also been to jail a couple times for drug parifanellia and drug posession, the same day he arrived in florida my mom told us not to worry because we were leaving soon. later that night he and my stepfather had gotten drunk, he was cool as long as things went his way. He later learned that my mom and aunt wasn't going to be supplying there habbits as they were trying to free them selves from drugs, when my dad got drunk he was very loud and stupid and sometimes he could be very scary. he used to send me to the store for him to purchase cigaretts, Kool filter kings them were his favorite when he could afford them or if someone offered to buy him some, when he made me wash the dishes he would make me wash the spoons and forks first and then the cups and glasses then the bowls and the plates the pots and pans was last, I used to be tired and if I didnt wash a dish right he made me rewash all of them, to make a long story short he could be an ass hole at times. Things went so wrong when he came down to florida, He started calling everyone out of their names, Everyone he talked to was a bitch or a hoe, he was waiting on the perfect moment to disrespect my mom so he just looked at her with a mean mug. the next day my stepfather snapped, and started beating my mom because she left him in cincinnati and everytime he thought about it he beat her he still did drugs and was drinking bad now the aunts boyfriend is also beating her. its a total of nine minor children in the house. the aunts boyfriend was something else to. my stepfather kept trying to get my mom to leave florida and go back to Cincinnati, my mom refused . . . while my mom and aunt were at work my stepfather and uncle was Skeaming, and because I used to urinate on myself from all the nightmares of bing so frightend of what the strange man had done to me at seven years old, and the abuse I went through with my stepfather I was afraid to go to the bathroom in the middle of the night. my stepfather would ask me if I had pissed on myself. he would make me take off my underwear and where them like a hat all day and when I thought things could get worse, he would verbally abuse me. he sexually assulted me when no one was around, he made me take off my underwear in front of him, it was so damn uncomfortable. the next day if I peed on myself he would say drop them draws you know the routine. I said, " no I didnt pee." scared and shaking . . . Just then my uncle came in the room they had been drinking they sent the other kids outside they took the matress off the bottom bunk and they made me take my clothes off while laughing at each other while calling me name. they tied me up by my arms and legs with tube socks to the bottom bunk bed they beat me until I couldnt cry nomore. that same night my stepfather came into the room where I was sleeping and put his hands down my pants he my rubbing my private area . . . when I woke up I tried to yell stop but he quickly put his hand over my mouth and told me to shut the fuck up. when he told me to shut the fuck up he told me to lay the fuck back down. he left the room because he heard movement in the hallway. it was his sister, she saw him and asked, "what are you doing ?" he said, "i was checking to see if Tip pissed on her self." she said, "oh" I just layed there and cryed. my mom would call Cincinnati to ask family if they can stop by her house to see if her checks came because they were not coming to Florida. They would call Later and tell her no they wasnt there. she called the government and they said that someone called using her information and had them resend to Cincinnati at the old address, mom said they were supposed to be coming here so they put a security code on the account so that if the person that called before calls back and dont know the answer they would not get any information. Then they reissued the check that was missing, mom went to visit cincinnati and she discovered that a couple of her family members was cashing her checks and spent them. but while in cincinnati my mom was trying to find us another apartment so she could leave my stepfather down in florida she found one and paid the rent and deposit, she came back and washed up everything we had and bagged it up she sat it outside in the garage, the next day she went to work like usuall her and my aunt, my step father and uncle found a job at some place doing construction, they didnt come home till about twelve at night mom got off at four she quickly hugged my aunt and told her that she was saving money to move back to cincinnati, tuff as life was for a eight year old I knew I had to remain strong for the younger kids but it was hard when you had two peopl attacking you. my uncle used to force me to suck his penis and when I refuse he would say ima kick yo ass or if I told he would hurt me, I never felt so low down in all my life he forced himself in my mouth one day and made me vomit he got mad because it got on him, so he whooped me and when he was asked why I had gotten into trouble he would say cause she hid some pissy painties or because he asked me to do something and I didnt do it, I was so hurt and afraid that I couldnt tell any one and when I tried to get close to my aunt to tell her wut her brother and babydaddy done one of them would enter the room where we was. but moving on one night my aunt couldnt take it anymore so she told my uncle and my dad to get out her house. her and my uncle start arguing her beat her so bad then my mom and stepfather started fighting. my uncle grabbed a metal table leg off the table that was already broken he hit my aunt upside the head with it right between the eyes she grew an instant knot. my stepfather done threw my mom down thirteen steps. I was scared so I ran for the phone, my aunt ran in the kitchen beside me she had stabbed herself in the abdomen with a barbaque fork, it had a long brown handle, I couldnt believe my eyes. the police finally came and took the fork from my aunts hand as she laid on the floor my mom rushed in to see wut happened and my uncle was already gone, my dad was leaving out another door, the fire department came and asked wut happened nobody knew it but me, so I told them about the fighting and how she stabbed herself in front of me, I still couldnt believe it I was in shock. a few days later my mom picked her check and cashed it, my grandmother even sent money to us through western union. my aunt had came home from the hospital, she thanked me for saving her life. my mom told my stepfather and the others that was in the house that she was taking for a walk to the store and that she would be back, we left out there was a cab at the garage we helped remove or clothes out the garage and mom rushed and closed the trunk we got into the cab and drove off to the grey hound we were going, when we got there the bus for cincinnati had just pulled up. mom got our luggage out the cab and we got on the bus and cinncinati here we come. the bus ride made us tired when we got in the station mom called a cab, "where are we going I asked" "home she said", we pulled up at this big building on a dead end street, we had never gotten to experiance our home without a guy for a while. but mom was really tired she had gotten a temperary restaining order on my step father and that kept him away, when I was twelve years old my mom thought she had met the perfect guy, "michael smith" he was loving and caring in the begining. he pretended that he was hardworking, even though he drank he pretended it was only a small amount. there wasnt a sighn in the begining that he was an alcoholic or that there was any drug use, he never done drugs with me and my siblings around he started talking about he was our new daddy and we supossed to call him daddy, we laugh cause we thought it was funny but he was dead serious he said if we didnt we would be punished severly, my mom had been with him now for five months she was trying to work a couple hours a day so she could make extra money and one day I was sent home from school he was at the house im guessing he answered the phone and pretended to be my daddy or something because soon as I walked in the house he said you might as well gone in your room and take your clothes off, the teacher just called me and your about to get yo ass whooped, I used the bathroom and locked my self in my room I even moved the dresser in front of the door so if he picked the lock he still couldnt get in, he finanlly came and couldnt get in he said open this fucking door I said hell naw he said ooh ima woop your ass when you come out I said and ima tell my daddy, he said tell your daddy bitch he dont want you yo momma got me. my mom just got in the house she said what the fuck is going on I opened the door, and said the school called and sent me home and he go say I might as well take my clothes off he was bouta beat me so I locked my door, my momma said oh naw boo you aint going to woop my child we just met and they dont need a daddy they got one, he said bitch wut am I hear for then I was smiling cause mom had spoken up this time and I was proud of her, she said I dont care why your hear you not about to put yo hands on my kids thats what im here for. she had rented a sterio and a livingroom suit and washer and dryer he stole it all when we was gone one day, we came home he had broke in and stolen it the neighbors said he said its ok she moving. my mom called the police and reported that he had stolen her stuff she also called the rent a center, and showed the the report the brung her some more items, and the police was looking for him, my mother continued to see him on the down low. He would take her down his sisters house to spend the night she was always partying drinkin smoking and playing cards, she cooked all the time, I met her once when they were together, mom had spent the night down there with him it was cold outside to being around thanksgiving time, when she came home the next day she had a black eye and a busted mouth she said he showed off on her while he was with his people because of her defending me when he was trying to woop me for getting suspended. she made the decission to stop dealing with him. so a couple days later he tried to come over and mom didnt open the door. we looked at him out the window and laughed, he threw up the middle finger at us, and that was the last of him. At thirteen years old there was a women that lived on the same street as us but further down, Her name was ms lisa she was a grown person dream she sold everything the grown ups needed, she sold pills, liquor, beer, food, pops, she even had card games and domino tournaments, when mom discovered this she was there everyday her and my mom became close friends mom had a tab that she never paid . . . we walked over ther one time her house was full of smoke thy were partying in front of her house the music was playing in there cars and they were laughing loud. I asked her if my mom was there she said no but she left the keys for yall and she handed them to me, thank you I said. we went in the house and cleaned up we fixed something to eat mom had went shopping, she retuned about three hours later and she was empressed. about six months later my mom was visiting ms lisa and her nephew phill had just gotten out of jail. so mom was attracted to him he was light skinned and thick in the shoulders, he had that fresh out of jail glow he was about thirty years old I think my mom was about thirtyfour years old ms lisa had introduced them to each other, my mom didnt even know what he went to jail for she never asked, all she knew was he was a nice looking man. she was visiting ms lisa more just to see him and he didnt visit everyday but the last time he came to ms lisa house my mom and him start talking and kissing ms lisa said aight now yall better be ready to pay each other tabs, one day my mom brung tony to the house for dinner to meet us I aint no what to think of him because at this point I felt all men was the same he had to show us he was the one. this man just got done doing ten years in jail he walked on his tip toes, and I didnt trust him, Now its only been about two weeks since he has been out of jail and ms lisa called my mom and I answered the phone she asked me if tony was there I said yes hold on when tony got the phone he left out very fast my mom followd him and because I was nosey I followed along. pretending I was playing outside she said you bastard she asked my mom to go to the store for her she went and I stayed behind when mom get down the street I walked over to the door and heard her saying you stole a bottle of vodka lastnight you owe me twenty dollars and a hundred dollars on yo tab he said ok ima pay you when she get her check she said she owe me fifty already, he said ok well will give you half then the other half when we get some more money, now im thinking how can you decide how to spend my moma money. as I sat on the steps in front of her house im still listening she said and you know you cant be up there with that lady and she got kids. I ran to meet my mom and told her everything she said ok im ask him about it when he by himself. now has already caught feelings for this man they already had sex and im thirteen im not dumb, so when she asked him why was he in jail he said some body accused me of molesting there child. she asked if he had done it he said hell naw thats my family so she believed him, he said that side of the family never liked him anyways so they made up anything to get him in trouble, mom continued to see him and on the thirteenth day we came home from school and mom told us that they went to the justic of peace and gotten married . . . she barely knew this man, only from what he told her. he didnt even have a job. after they got married he started being creepy he laughed at everything he started eating up Everything, his whole demeaner changed after the second day he would be creeping around sometime we wouldnt hear him come in a room we would just look up and there he was, ms lisa tried to tell my mom that he wasnt the guy for her. he started drinking heavily and doing drugs he was hiding it well at first then he and mom would do drugs together, he faught my mom every other day and each time he would say he's sorry and that it would never happen again she thought that because this was her husband she had to put up with it. one day a neighbor had given us a puppy because we played with their puppy everyday, well we thought it was a puppy it was full grown and pregnant, when they brung us the puppy we were so happy we played and fed him everyday we used to ride this grey hound in florida he was a big dog he would let us climed up on him and ride him like a horse we had fun. but one day after school we couldnt find our puppy and here comes tony with this suitcase he said open it he stood back and it was our puppy we cried and cried he done killed the dog, tony was laughing with this creepy laugh as if he was crazy. Finally mom said she couldnt do it so she broken things off with tony, she told him he had to go, and he did we hadnt heard or seeen tony for about three months. when he came back he was trying be nice by doing things around the house he had given the boys a hair cut and he evn offered to shape me up, he cut all my hair off around my hairline I had to wear a hooded jacket for weeks until my hair grew back I was pissed and after he was done he started laughing my mom even laughed. well mom has moved again, mom and tony still drunk and did drugs they still faught or should I say tony still faught my mom, foolishly my mom moved right next door to another liquor lady. This time the lady lived right next door, we were side by side but this time we were in another house and not an apartment. when my stepfather found out my mom was married he was mad as ever cause he knew his chances of getting back together with my mom was gone, living at the new house we had two dogs a girl rotweiler and a boy. We watched them grow up we had a yard with a chain link fence in the front and back. mom put tony out again one day for stealing money from her was laying the yard yelling shugga I love you. we would look out the window and mess with him by dropping stuff on him from the window ceil, there was rusted nails, drywall peices and other things he would jump and dust him seflf off like a spider was crawling on him, we would jump out the window and laugh. we sprayed water on him from an old windex bottled he thought it was raining he would say shugga can I come back in please its raining. when he discoverd that we were the ones droping things he said can you get your kids plz they throwing shit out the window. she would yell up stairs yall better lay down we giggled then too. he finally made his way back in the house, and when he did he acted like he wanted to play with us so he start popping us with this long plastic yellow bat my brothers had. he chased us threw the house he even chased my mom to, then he started hitting us to hard. My mom said thats enough now shit, but he kept on playing and we running and crying he was paying us back for messing with him the day before, soon had pulled out this mass (pepper-spray) and chased us we hid behind the doors thinking he couldnt find us, he start spraying through the cracks and laughing. We were crying now forreal it burned he done massed everybody we all running falling trying to find the bathroom. after it was clear we stopped playing me and my brother said we was going to get his punk ass back so when he left we searched high and low for this mass we finally found it in my moms room in her dresser. When he returned later that day he got drunk and went to sleep. good thing my momma went to the bathroom we srayed him right in the face he was dripping wet. that was for everybody we threw the mass in the back alley . . . lol . . . the next day we was waiting to see what trick he had up his sleeves, he was cool doe he stayed in the house the whole day, he didnt have money for drugs so mom cooked we ate and all went to sleep, we was awaken by this loud dragging noise tony was dragging our tv out the house, it was a big name brand floor model tv. mom was yelling what are you doing bring that back here he was steady dragging my mom said im bouta call the police he took off running, we had to help mom drag it back in the house and only getting half way through to the house here comes tony with two other dude's my mom said where yall going they said tony sold us this tv and we paid him. My mom said I dont know why because this my dam tv and he was just stealing it out my house so I held up the telephone and said I was about to call the police, the guys left and didnt come back. the next day tony came back and he acted as if nothing had happened him and my mom argued then he hit her, me and my brother sent little kids up stairs we was about to help momma this time. we snuck outside and got these two sticks we sat back there for this occasion, we started hitting tony he was running and trying to get us mom was yelling yall stop I can take care of myself. tony snatched the stick from my brother and was trying to swing at him I swung my stick with all my might and hit tony in back of the head. he ducked I snatch the other stick and gave it back to my brother. Tony got the message not to fuck with our mom. so he chilled out, the next day we left out for school I had skipped school over my aunts house I told her wut had happened she was like wut I wish I was there. I left the kitchen window unlocked for the other kids they knew if no one was home to climbed in the window. but sitting at my aunts house school had just let out my mom came in my aunts house her face was messed up, What happened to you I ask she was crying. She said tony punched her with all his might because she wouldn't lay down, he hit her a few times bacause her lip was messed up to. I called the police and they came and took pictuers they put a search out for him cause she filed charges, her eye was damaged the doctor had to hold her eye up with a metal plate. we havent seen or heard from tony in months we assumed he was in jail by now but they never caught him because he went to stay with his sister in kentucky. it was about 9pm tony came knocking he could have killed my mom she has seizures real bad, my mom had a restaining order on him so he wasnt supposed to be knocking at the door my mom said you better leave I yelled before I call the police we called my uncle he came right away tony ran off yelling im sorry shugga I love you, my uncle chased him for two blocks. he told us if he come back call me ima beat his punk ass. we laughed and went in the house my uncle left so mom locked all doors and windows. we never seen or heard frm him again and moma finally got a divorce from this dude. so from being mistreated so much while I was growing up I had became self conscious as I started growing breasts and pubic hairs in places I tried to hide myself under baggy clothes so boys wouldnt look at me. I wouldnt go to any pool parties because I felt exposed in a swimming suit. I really didnt interact with to many family members . . . the only people I really felt comfortable being myself around was with my younger siblings . . . I did enjoy it when my mom would give us money to go skating with some of the kids in the neighborhood. I was not into talking to boys I was afraid that they would hurt me for the longest time when I was growing up I met this one guy and hadn't met any one like him yet I loved him so much, I stop talking to him because I was embarressed when he ask to visit my house, I knew I couldnt take him there because my house wasnt up to pare like his his mothers house was nice she had a job and went to work everyday. mom had told us that a family member had told her if she didnt get her act together they was calling 241 kids, she said she loved us and that she wanted to check herself into rehab. so she went and made arangments to check her self in, and when the case worker came to the house there wasnt a problem but my mom had mentioned even though she had food and clean clothes and things for the kids that she needed help to stop drinking, she stated that she had already checked herself into rehab she just need somebody to watch the kids. thats a great idea the worker said, do you have family that can take the kids he called a numerious amount of family had all said no they cant watch us, so we were splitten up and placed into differant foster homes I was so hurt that nobody in our family would take us in not even those that pretended to love us, the family that I was placed with had already had a foster son there he was about eight years old so he reminded me of my baby brother cause he barely talked he was very shy, the foster mother was trying to make jokes to make me feel welcomed but I was so upset that I wanted to go home that I never found anything funny, she intoduced me to her own daughter who didnt live there but she stopped by to do laundry . . . she took me in the back and showed where my room would be, there was clean linen on the beds the room smelled nice and clean the sheets looked like they were ironed on the beds it was light blue and crispy clean so I sat on the bed and they walked out, I think I was only there for about two days when the step mother called her daughter and asked if she could come sit with us while she ran some arronds, the daughters who's name was sheena came over about twenty minutes later, the daughter was gay and she was dressed like a boy the first day I met her and she was dressed like a boy this time around to, she kept watching me. When the mother returned she saw I was still in my room she asked if I was hungary, I said no mam may I use your phone to call my mom she had given me this number to call her when I needed to talk to her so I called my mom and talked to her for about an hour then the foster lady said I had to get off the phone, So I told my mom I loved her and that I had to go, mom said ok call me tomorrow. I hung the phone up and sat at the kitch table the foster lady sat at the table with me, she was asking wut school I attended and if I had any brothers and sisters. I told her my school name and that I had two brother and two sisters then she said why did you have to come here and I explained to her the reason why and I also told her that we get to go back home, she said yes but no time soon your mom is in a ninety day program. I cried again because that was to long I was fifteen yrs old and I wasn't staying at this women's house no three months, I hated my family how could they abandon us the way they did. well I have now been in this house for four days and this ladys daughter has begun to get on my last nerve talking about how cute I was and if I had a boyfriend or girlfriend, I said why would I have a girlfriend thats nasty, she said I was just askin I said well stop talkin to to me, I closed my room door wher I stayed for three more days I didnt want to eat when they offered me something when the girl left the women said honey you have to eat would you like a bacon sandwhich, "yes mam I would so I ate the sandwhich, she mad a phone call asking her daughter not to forget to come over after work so she could go to bingo. after eating I went in my room and took a nap, when I woke up the foster lady was getting ready to leave I walked out my room and into the kitchen she was telling sheena to feed me because all I ate was breakfast. when the women left her daughter told me she had a crush on me, I said thats not normal she said I know I was born like this she asked if she can I kiss me, uugghh no I said aint you grown she said im only twenty and im only fifteen. I went in my room and layed on the bed she came in five minutes later talking about I was going to be with her she was laying on me and trying to hold me down I just remember fighting with all my might, I finally was free I ran out the door and towards the bus stop I had about two dollars the worker had given me, I jumped on the bus crying and breathin fast I aint no where my younger siblings was all I remember doing was going back to my mom's house, I called my mom and told her wut happen she called the social worker and he came to the house. He asked me wut happened and I told him. he went over and asked them wut happen, they lied and said I attacked the girl cause I wanted to go home he said he knew they was lien because the mom and the daughter gave two differant stories, but any way he told me that he had gotten a call from my stepfather's relative and that she would take us in, I was happy he said he was going to pick up my younger siblings and then he would be back to get me, then he left he came back around an hour ina half later and drove us to the aunts house my brother and sister was so happy to see me, we was just happy to be together. the hcjafs worker thought this was a perfect environment. because she had a house he just kept saying how we would enjoy living here. this relative only wanted us because the goverment would issue her a check she hadnt had nothing to do with us any other time. she was happy to see us while the worker was there, After the worker left she started mistreating us. she only fed us once a day twice if she was in a good mood, she received vouchers from the government to purchase clothing and the other things we needed and instead of her buying the things we needed, she decided to buy things her kids needed instead she bought my sister a couple things she wanted my sister and her youngest daughter to dress alike. she abused me because I was trying to defend myself and my younger siblings, she talked to us like were crazy she allowed her eldest daughter whom was about twentyfive years old to punch my baby sister in the face and when I tried to help her she held me back saying if I was to do anything. she would send us back where we came from and I didnt want us to be split up so I didnt do anything, also when her daughter was there they would smoke marijuana rolled up in a white paper called tops, they called it smoking a joint she would let her daughter disrespect us by saying things like thats a dam shame they momma aint want them or I know yall better not fuck up my mommy house or momma why did you take in them raggedy ass kids. she locked us in the basement for hours whenever she had company, She didnt want anyone to know we was there when her landlord came for repairs she sent us in the basement and told us not to make any noise or we would be sent off. We used to laugh at her because she was a heavy women and she would stomp as she walked across the floor we would say she was going to fall in through the ceiling. Why would she mistreaat us the way if she aint want us then why allow the worker to leave us there, she made us clean up her whole house while her and her kids just sat back and watched us, when she fed us she always said eat slow cause you will stay full longer, she gave us water with everything, on the day she made us clean the basement was enough for me I asked my younger brother and sister was they going to leave with me if I run away they said yes, my lil brother was just smiling away so her youngest daughter sold candy bars for the school and I used to watch where she put the money, She counted two hundred and fourty dollars and put it in a yellow envelope on her dresser underneath a stack of books and papers, so when she went to school she left the money there and I was actin like I was about to throw away some trash to open the door because she yelled about us opening the door. Soon as I got the money I told my siblings to come on my baby brother was scared and he didnt want to leave so I hugged him and kissed him I told him ill be back for him he said ok. we left and that night we were upset because we had to leave my lil brother so we went back around the time we knew he was outside playing I yelled at him he ran to me he said she wooped him for telling that we had left, so we ran and jumped on the metro bus and headed home, we stopped at the store and bought food with the money I stolen from my cousin. At the store we bought snacks, pop, pickles, lunchmeat and bread and cheese we had cearl and milk, and ramien noodles, I bought hotpockets and other stuff for the microwave. we went in the house through the back door im glad I had left it unlocked. we locked all doors and windows put the food in the refridgerator and got some snacks and went up stairs, I made sure the curtains were pulled over the windows so no one could look in and I made sure the lights was off on the first floor so no one knew we were there. I made sure we ate something every day, mom had to do fifteen more days of treatment. the police came by the house to take us back to the relatives house but we didnt open the door, we watched tv and was laughing at them knocking on the door. the next day the worker knocked onthe door we knew he would take us back so we didnt answer for him either. and a few days later we lost count of how many days till mom came home, when the worker came back he said Tip I know yall in there open the door I wont take yall back so I opened the door he came in he saw we was eating he said why did yall run, I explained everything my sister showed him her eye and I showed him the bruises on my legs and back, he was furious he wrote down things and took pictures, we told him she wouldnt feed us and that she locked us in the basement she bought her kids clothes with our vouchers because she said that we wasnt going to be wearing new clothes and her kids wasnt. just then guess who came in the door my mom oh we were so happy to see her we hugged her and almost made her fall. she picked up my lil brother and said hey big boy I miss you she was all clean and pretty she had her hair done, she asked why was we there, the worker explained he even said I done a good job at protecting us just never do that again because its dangerous. he then took us to get our things from the relative house she brung our bags outside he said wut is this aint this the same stuff I dropped off, oh god she continued to say she was nervous and shaking bad like she was having a seizure the worker said where is ther clothes for three months you better go get every piece of it right now or im calling the police. oh god she said as she went inside and brung out a few more things we said we know where they are he followed us inside the house he said get everything that supossed to be yalls. we took new socks out the drawers, and new underclothes all the stuff she bought her kids with them vouchers we took back. When I was a child I was afraid of the dark for a long time, it seamed that the bad things would only happen once the lights were out I was so afraid that someone was going to come in and kill me. I never tried to fight back when I was being abused, I had taken so much and so many differant kinds of abuse that I almost started to give up. I was really waiting on the lights to come on in my own life. I used to think I was ugly or maybe it was because I was concidered poor, I couldnt understand how I was everyone's target . . . why? me why am I constantly reminded of my hurt everyday, I remained a victim for so long that I became numb to feelings and pain. I think I became amuned to whoopings my mom used to say oh it dont hurt then she started punching me, I kept things bottled up for a long time when we visited a relative's house that we were close to, we were allowed to walk around freely and interact with others but we werent allowed to do that at home. Home was supposed to be a peaceful place, your supposed to feel loved and protected and I felt neither, I was very observant I looked around alot and I always paid attention to my younger brothers and sister. I made sure I cleaned up after my siblings where ever we were, I didnt want anybody to say nothing bad and I didnt want to wear out our welcome I was trying to show our appreciation for inviting us. some people saw us as a burden so they talked about us, its hard to sit or walk pass someone and you hear them say here go shugga (my-mom) and them bad ass kids, and soon as we enter the house we was told not to bother nothing. I always thought we acted like normal kids people just wanted something to say because they didnt like my mom so they took it out on her kids, my mom didnt care to much about what people said about her because that only gave us something to talk about when we went home. In every family there is one nosey aunt or uncle who loves to stir up trouble always made a big deal out of a little situation, I had a aunt that tried to fight everybody when she start drinking. When a person drinks it gives them courage to speak how they really feal, they say a drunk thought is a sober thought. I got an uncle that tells corny jokes when he start smoking marijuana, if he drank he would follow people around talking to himself and the first person that said anything to him he would stand next them and hold a conversation until he realize that they were not interested he would walk off talking shit, When he found a comfortable spot to sit he would take his shoes off that let us know he wasnt getting back up so we would sit down and listen to his corny stories, he would fall asleep in the middle of a conversation, we were kids so we would rub feathers in his ear and watch him smack his self in the ear and face we would run and laugh. we used to watch my uncles dance they would play Michael Jackson music they would mimick the michael jackson dance moves and we all clap and cheer them on. once I became interested in boys I was fifteen years old and there was this one boy that was very popular in school he had all the ladies wanting to be his girlfriend all the girls was all over him, I was about the only girl that didnt pay him much attention because I didn't dress like the other kids I didnt wear the name brand shoes other kids wore I had to make my own style with wut I had, I was clean and I tried to keep my hair done. I didnt have many accesories like the other girls, thats why I never said anything to him, I thought he wouldn t be interested in me, And little did I know he was very interested . . . he stopped me in the hallway after lunch and I was on my way to the restroom and he said aye excuse me let me talk to you when you come out, ok I said. so I finished and washed my hands I made sure I didnt have a boogie in my nose and I walked out smiling. He said out of all these girls that try and talk to me your the only one that dont. I said its because of all them girls being on you thats the reason why I didn't say anything. he said he said I like you. he wrote his number down and handed it to me and said call me later. he ran to class and I went to my class. I didnt call him later and the next day I stopped by my aunts house in the morning and put on one of her jean outfits and accesories and sprayed some of her perfume and I walked on to school. the guy I met was standing outside the school building talking to another guy, as I pretended not to see him he saw me, he walked up on me and hugged me all the way inside the school building, he said why you aint call me lastnight I said I forgot because we went to my grandmother house and I couldnt talk. all the other girl was upset they rolled there eyes and tryed to fight me. so after he went to class I was approached by a couple girls in the hallway and one of the girls said I hope you dont think thats your boyfriend or nothing, cause somebody else likes him, so I said well if he liked them he woulda spoken to them. She couldnt say nothing else but well ill see you after school, I was a little scared because I didnt know any of the girls well enough to feel as if one them had my back. I didnt have any family there, after school all the girls was crowed around in a circle as I walked out some girl yelled there she go. my cousin crystal had walked to the school to meet her friend and she seen me and ran over yelling hell naw thats my cousin the guy that was trying to talk to me ran over and said hell naww yall aint bouta fight her wuts up, he grabbed me and we walked off. I looked back they was salty, the next day no one said anything to me I was able to walk home in peace, after school he asked me if I wanted to walk to his house I said yes! so we walked he introduced me to his mom and sister and his brothers, it was ok him mom was cooking, I sat outside with him in his back yard and there was a small boy around ten years old he was popping popers that go inside a cap gun with a lighter, and I was jus watching him because he was standing next to me he was too close so I just scooted back some and he smacked me in the face and asked me what I was looking at, I got up and chased him and I was pulled by the colar by my boyfriend he was yelling no stop! he grabbed me so hard that I slid and fell on the damp grass" I went straight home my boyfriend aint know my number and I wasnt going to call him. I was through talking to him the next day at school he said I was trying to tell you not to hit that lil boy he is adhd and his daddy is a police officer and they just let the lil boy do anything he wanted and if you would have hit him they probally would have tried to put you in jail. oh ok I said and we were still dating for about three months his mom decided to move and we lost touch, so I didnt want another boyfriend because I liked him. I had gotten into it with my mom and she scratched me up, I never hit her back cause she was my mom she put me out the house I slept out side for two weeks in an abandon apartment I didnt have any friends so I couldnt ask to spend the night, know one ever knew because I would wash up in the bathroom of every place I went to whether it was the gas station or just to drop by a relative house I would to pretend to have to use the restroom and I would wash up real quick but I cleaned up after myself my relative didnt know I was homeless but just so happend to ask me if I was hungary and if I wanted to stay for dinner and I was so happy I even stayed the night that night. I couldnt take it any more I went to the federal building and told the represenative that I need to speak to some one right away. when I finally spoken with some one I informed the lady that my mom was getting my money and wasnt giving me anything out my check I told them that I slept outside for two weeks and I need my money the lady walked away and came back later she gave me a check with my name on it. when I left I went to my sister house she had gave me her last twenty dollars she took me to the bmv and helped me get a I.D I was so happy. I cashed the check and went apartment hunting and lucked up on one, it wasnt equipt with a stove and a refridgrator I had to furnish it myself so I passed on that and went a little further I finally found one about the houses down away from my mom, I was happy my mom was pissed that she aint get my check for the next month. I went to rent a center and got me a bedroom suit and a living roomsuit and a kitchen table set, I was very proud of myself. my rent was one hundred and ninty dollars and the deposit was waved so I was doing ok now I had to spend my last two hundred dollars on food and I had fifty dollars left for the household items. I finally went over to my moms house and told her I live next door she was ok with it, we tried to establish a friendship, me and my baby brother was best friends he always came to visit me he helped me alot because he had two jobs. I had started to spend time with this guy he used to pay me just to ride around and talk he just wanted to be in the company of a women he gave me about twelve hundred one time just to ride with him and pick up office supplies. I was excited to have met this guy cause he didn't want sex he just wanted a friend. when he dropped me off he said ill be back in town before thanksgiving ill see you then, ok I said I went in the house because it was ten o clock pm. the next day I got ready to wash my clothes and decided to go shopping and buy me some clothes because I didnt have many, I was going to wash later so I got the clothes out and put them in the kitchen on the floor beside the table my brother came and ask me to wash his clothes too so I said ok we had been smoking marijuna and we were high, he left out to get his clothes and I went to the fridge to get a drink cause I was thirsty I grabbed a cup and proceeded to pour until my brother hit the door real hard he was letting me know that his clothes was at the door instead of sitting them inside the door he was late for work and his ride was outside I spilled the juice it had over flowed from the cup, it was everywhere I had a large picture someone gave me of jesus hanging in my kitchen it matched the room, so I looked up at it while the juice was spilling and I thought I was tripping from being high "jesus had turned his head and said huury and get it up, I used the clothes from the floor that I was about to wash and wiped up the spill, I looked again and this time he said go check on your mom now I really thought I was tripping so I went to knock on my mom door and she was coming out. I didnt get to knock because she was already on her way to me, I said "mom are you okay" "yeah" she answered, she said Tip I was just hemeraging real bad in the bathroom I applied pressure with some tissue and it stopped. I said momma I think I just saved your life, she said wut are you talking about so I told her to follow me to my house, I showed her everything and told her I think the red juice was supposed to be your blood. She was in shocked like thats why you came down and asked me was I okay, "yes mam". and we still talks about that to this day. My lil brother had already went to work but we told him soon as he gotten off, since I been out on my own I havent looked back. my life has just begun and im determined to run til my legs fall off, My mother knew many many people and those that knew her knew she can be sweet at times, my mother had men friend everywhere and they didnt mind giving my mom money and gifts, it was numerious accassions when iv'e witnessed gentlemen handing her wads of cash, now there was this one guy I would consider to be the only real friend she had he owned a used furniture store, he would pick us up and take us groccery shopping take us to his house and let us wash our clothes, and he pretty much too us and picked us up from any where we went whenever my mom needed him he was there she would go over his house and help him clean up, his house was full of furniture and old radios, and clocks that people would drop off for him to fix, his store was so full of things he had no room for nothing or no one hahahaha ill wash the dishes for him and sweep the floor we would got to the store for him when ever he need us to. He had a trait in his throat and at first it was hard to understand him but being around him we learned quick, he was like our dad foreal he helped us with school work and fieldtrips, and one day he got his leg amputated and had to use crutches to get around, He was sad after that and you can tell in his spirits that he was self consious about going out in public so whenever we was out and about he would always send one of us in the store or to put the letter in the mailbox and things like that we loved him. one day I came home from school and my mom and my lil brother was crying she said mr plill had died and how she found him in his house dead at the bottom of the steps, she said he called for her to come over earlier at a certain time she said when she got there he wrote a note saying that he felt sick and he left her things he wanted her to take home, I was so hurt behind that I didnt want to believe he was dead until I went to the funeral, At the funeral I wasnt even scared to see him I went up to him and cried like he was my daddy I held his hand and talked to him I asked him why did he leave me, and I told him that I need him I kissed his forhead and let him know I loved him and I thanked him for everything that he did for us and my mom. after the funeral his only living brother walked over to us and handed my mom the keys to mr phil's house he said he wanted me to give you these he said go over there and take whatever you wanted but make sure you clean up after yourself and lock the door, he said I have a set of keys ill come by in a couple days and finish the job. When we went home that day after the coffin was put in the ground we went home and cried. I was sad because I missed him asking me to put my mom on the phone. my mom had got his washer and dryer amung other things everytime she used them she thought of phil. RIP-PHILL . . . when I was going to school some teachers were cruel and didnt really wanna teach they was just there to be in competition with the other teachers, the teachers that liked you passed you and those that didnt also passed you so they wouldnt have to deal with you next year. you had to fit in with the popular crowd, kids are cruel they say things sometimes that they dont meen, for the holidays we had to stay home most christmas's because we didnt get anything new we had to stay in the house for a few days after christmas, but kids were so nosey and so cruel they teased us and made us feel bad by bragging about the things they got and askin us wut we go we would lie and say a new video game system with new games to play. I learned that when the seasons change people change, mom asked me one day where was I going I said down moochie house who was my favorite aunt, why should an inocent child have to remember any bad things in life although trials come "a child's life is wut the parents make it they shouldn't have to worry about grown up problems, I remember having to go to school just to eat for the day. and on the days that I wasnt in school, my mom took us to the soup kitchen to eat it was St Francis Seraph, it sat on the corner of liberty and vine street they welcomed and was open to anyone, it wasnt just my mom and her kids in the line it was a relative and her six children too. we used to have to stand in line and wait till they opened, we used to hide behind people when some one we knew would walk pass, we used to have fun after we went in and ate, we would grab alot of the stale loafs of bread they had sitting out for people to take home for free, we would have bread fights in there parking lot lol we had some good time's there were other children who paticipated. we made it a tradition to meet every thursday just so we could have a bread fight we would talk smack to each other all week as if we were winning a prize haha we even picked teams, The girls against the boys, those were the good old days. man being in high school was no walk in the park though I remember when my mom was sick on drugs and she went to the freestore for any and every thing she could find bring back or carry, she found clothes and shoes and belts and rings and all sorts of things, but kids wern't stupid they said we smelled bad. they talked about us so bad they said we found our clothes in the garbage can, my mom didnt care she washed and starched everything, as long as yall clean hell with wut somebody else gotta say. when I was younger and growing up I felt that I had to many responsabilities I just wanted to be a kid, we moved again closer to my dad I used to sit in the front of the house and just watch everything that was going on I used to hear someone talkin to me but I never paid much attention because it sounded like somebody was using a telephone. but one day I was sitting there and I heard the ladys voice again she said excuse me young lady I looked around she said im here in the window she said how are you I said im ok how are you she lived on the first floor of our building and we lived on the second floor, she said every time I see your looking sad, why do you look so sad I said im not sad she said if not sad who hurt you. she was an older women she had a very heavyset build she had coustody of her grandaughter whom was about three years old, she said I know you dont know me and you dont have to talk to me but I need a friend and if you ever want to talk im here. she said ill give the best advice that I can, I went upstairs and the next day when I came outside that lady was in the window she said my name is ms felicia, can you asked your mom if you can go to the store for me. ok I ran up stairs and asked mom if I can go to the store for the lady on the first floor, she said yeah and hurry up back, I went down stairs and said my mom let me go I said my name is Tip. she said nice to meet you Tip thats a pretty name she said my grandaughter name is lona, she said im glad you came cause I been needing someone to go to the store for me and now I got you, I smiled thank she said I will pay you. she gave me a list of things dipers size five, milk, bread, butter, lunchmeat, crackers, sugar, half pound ground beef, and a box of cereal. I left and went down the street to IGA food store. and gotten everything on the list and took it back to ms felicia with her receipt, and when I handed her the bread she smiled and said wow its not smashed. she checked her change and looked at her receipt she then smiled again and handed me ten dollars I said thank you and I left out and went upstairs my babybrother was waiting to go outside so I helped him with his shoes, and my babysister was ready so I took them to the store and bought them whatever they wanted, my other brother was always running away and mom was getting tired of looking for him so she let him stay out most days until he came back on his own. so when we arrived at the house ms felicia wasnt in the window, we went upstairs and watched tv the tv show's we liked the most was the fresh prince of belair' and the other tv show's was the cosby show and family matters, we also would watch married with children. the next day on my way to school ms felicia was in the window, she said when you come from school can you go to the store for me. I said yes mam. and after school I ran in the house I asked can I go to the store for the lady on the first floor. and I took off running, she handed me a list and said I need you to get all these items. As I proceeded to leave she said please dont smash the bread, there was candy corn, two dollars worth of hot sauce meat, a loaf of bread, one pack of crackers, a gallon of juice, a two liter pepsi, and one pack of porkchops for ten dollars. and when I returned she said wow you didnt smash the bread. she checked her receipt and her change then she gave me thirteen dollars, I was happy and sleepy so went up stairs and took a nap. when I woken up my mom said ms felicia called for you . . . ok I went to see wut ms felica wanted she said did I give you a hundred dollar bill by mistake and I said ill go check I went upstairs and checked my shoe where I put my money before I took a nap, I checked my shoe and yes she did I found two hundred dollar bill's a ten and three single dollars bills, I didnt tell her about the two but I told her about the one ok she said I was makin sure I gave you one, I said wut is it for she said because I kno yall need grocceries up stairs and the thirteen dollars was for you. ok thanks so much, I went up stairs and looked in our fridge and she was right, I asked my mom when can we go shopping for food she said when I get my stamps in eighteen more days I said wut if I had some money to buy food can we go with you to buy food she said yes I went in my room and seperated the money I put my thirteen dollars under my bed matress, and took mom the two hundred dollar bills. she jump up I said shhh, she said where did you get this from I said ms felicia gave me one to buy food up here but she gave me two by mistake, mom said oh. lets go she locked the door and we went shopping at IGA mom groccery total was one hundred and fifty she said can she have the rest I said yeah long as we got food, some guy mom knew had given us a ride back home. we were happy mom yelled thank you ms felicia through her window. the next day felicia asked if I wanted to help her with a little housework I said yes I ran up stairs and asked mom if I could held the lady on the first floor she said hell yeah, and I ran down stairs I was washing the dishes and I swept the floor. my mom came down and knocked she opened the door she said I stopped by to say thanks and to make sure my daughter wasnt getting your nerves, "No" ms felicia said I really appreciate yo daughter I didnt have no body to help me before yall moved here, oh ok mom said well she will help you as long as she feels welcome she dont like to be overworked. ms felicia said ok Thank ms felicia said. mom left I said she wouldnt know wut overworked is as much as I clean up and wash upstairs, ms felicia said why wuts wrong I told her everything about me and wuts been going on she said im so sorry to hear that and im here for yall, she said im your new friend and your big sister she said ill never tell you nothing wrong, I will always expect you to do your best she said if you need help with homework ill help you. ms floura started cooking big dinners and sending food upstairs, we had began to have a relation like best friends would, I done her hair and polished her nails I would lay on her couch and tell her my million stories and she would always listen she told me what was right and wrong wut I should and shouldnt do she would also ask me if I had a boyfriend I said no she said good they aint about nothing she never cursed. one day ms floura told me she was moving to another state cause she was tired of being here her grandaughter mother walked pass everyday and never stopped by to see if she was alive. I was so hurt and two weeks later I came from school she was really gone I cried she didnt even say good bye. when I got up stairs my mom was high she said that lady downstairs brung a box of shit up here for you. I took the box in my room and sat on the bed I opened the box there was a couple shirts and a few pair of jeans for me she went and bought this stuff back to me she had a pair of shoes inside the box in it's original package the LA gear with the pretty shoestrings that I had been asking dad to buy she had a purse and perfumes and lotions and powder some earings and differant color acessories and some personal care items. she left a note saying I love you Tip and thank you for being there for me and my grandaughter would never forget you, look inside the purse she said its money for continuing to go to the store for me she said spend five dollars a day and dont etll your mom unless you want to. I put on the purse I didnt look inside to see how much money was in it it felt like alot but I showed mom all the stuff she bought me and the letter I stuck inside my back pocket,. aww that was nice my mom said, I finally locked my self in the bathroom and opened the purse there was an envelope with thirtyfive hundred dollar bills inside yes thirtyfive hundred dollar bills . . . I remember talking to ms felicia she said she had kept all her tax money for five years before she couldnt get around I just couldnt believe it. I counted it over and over again. I took twentyfive hundred and put it in the zipper part of my purse and started screaming like I just now opened the purse I torn up the letter and flushed it I came out the bathroom and sat at the table I said mom how much was the rent you owed, she said why you got some money if I had some how much do you need she said three hundred I counted from that thousand she said where did you get that from girl I said ms felicia put it in this purse. she said dam she loved you didnt she . . . mom eyes were big

I said how much was the gas and electric she said two hundred I counted that and then I said how much for the grocceries she how much you want it be I counted the last five and gave it her she was happy, she left to pay the bills and go shopping I went to the next corner after my mom left, with my brother and sister and bought them some shoes I counted four hundred before I left and put the rest up in the house I bought them some named brand shoes and a pair of socks. the total came up to a hundred and seventy five dollars I was only twelve. an out that four hundred I had two hundred, twenty five dollars left. I was proud we all had shoes then I turned around and bought my mom some shoes, she said she wore a size nine in women. we went in the house and put the shoe under the bed so mom couldnt see, when she came home she said come help me with the bags she showed me the rent receipts and the gas bill recipt. we were happy I saved the other money till it was really needed mom said I wish I could buy yall some shoes now I said, I already did. "what" she replied, I went and got the shoes, and even her shoes she was happy and she loved her nike air shoes. she said do you got any more money I said no how much was the food she said three hundred I kept the rest I said ok. she still aint know about the rest of the money she went out and checked the mailbox she said her go a letter from ms felicia I opened it at the table in front of my mom and siblings, ms felicia had wrapped up two thousand dollars in hundred dollar bills and said merry christmas! she had no return address so I couldnt say thank you. my mom started crying aww some body love us I handed my mom seventeen hundred and told her we need some clothes and buy the baby a toy or two. ima keep this three so mom didnt know I already had twentyseven hundred and sixty dollars hid in my room so I kept the three hundred seperate in case mom tried something sneaky . . . and she did after three weeks we had new clothes and shoes, she w¬s having company everyday and getting high that she came in my room and woke me up out my sleep and demanded that I give her that three hundred I kept saying no, and I didnt give it to her so she started punching me. I was hurt all I have done she was acting and treating me that way. the next day after she wasnt high she said im sorry baby for last nigh wut did I do. and I told her I save this money for us and you wanna spend it on your habbit thats not right I handed her two hundred and told her the last hundred is mine we need personal items ill start my period soon, but ms felicia sent me some in that big box, but mom said you right she had everything she needed. she didnt need nothing else. I got upset and went down my aunt house I took all my money out the house mom said I can go thats where I went sometimes to excape from people. she needed me any way she aint have no food or dipers for her babies she said she was waiting for her friend to come bring her some money she didnt know I had some and I didnt tell her until after the person came and left he gave her twenty dollars that wasnt enough for two kids so I went in the bathroom and gave two hundred dollars she asked where I get that money from I told her not to tell my mom I gave it to her and I didnt tell her about the rest. she was happy and asked me to watch the kids for her while she go to the store, and I sat there till she came back she did what she was supposed to do she even bought tissue she said thank you so much I said your welcome you always be helping me so I helped you . . . I went home before it got dark. my mom asked if I was ok I said yeah I gave my aunt that money so she could buy food she didnt have anything down there my mom said that was real nice of me. I still felt as if something was missing in my life so I asked my aunt if I could stay the weekend she said yes come on, so went down and I expressed my feelings to her I told her that I wanted to experiance picking out shirts with other girls my age and going to the movies going on dates with boys and etc. . . . she shared how she felt, we just had a bond that nobody could break she understood how I was feeling she said just be patient with mom she would be ok. I never had no one to nuture me and hold me and tell me everything would be okay, as I reached adult hood I was glad to know that I finally had some one who would love me and appreciate me for me, I am glad to announce to the World, that I had gotten married on March 6th 2003, I am also the proud mother of seven veautiful children. and I wasnt going to let nothing or no one hurt them, I want my children to grow up and dance like nobodys watching, sing like no one's listening, and love like nobody's been hurt. iv'e struggled with depression for many years and I never felt like hurting myself or other's I would run into my abusers not often but when I did I wanted to hurt them, but I knew there was no reward in that so I just continued to pray and ask God for strength. I never let one see me frowning and upset because then they would win by still thinking they had control over me. one of my younger brothers was incarcerated, and later released from prison he had to report to his probation officer every week, me and this brother never gotten along as we were growing up we just excepted each other because we had the same mother. he always ran away from home and was always doing bad things, his mantality was totaly differant from mine. he was a bloods gang leader and alot of people feared him . . . he had many friends that ran with him, he had that street life down pack he had just gotten out of jail and met this young lady he dated and they moved in together, he called me up on the telephone and asked me can he stay with me because some guys were he lived didnt like him they shot through the house while they were sleeping and the bullet hit the wall near the bed they slept in. I said yes you can stay but I have children and your friends are not welcomed in my home around my children, he agreed and said okay can I bring my girlfriend with me I dont wanna leave her down here so somebody can try to hurt her, I said ok now he didnt come that same day he came the following day, when he arrived he asked me if I knew anybody that sold weed. I said no because I dont smoke he said oh ok, he tried to call several people I guess he left to meet somebody with it, but when he came back he had some and my children was gone over there grandmother house for the weekend and im glad they were, I had my infant at home with me he was seven months old. two days latr my brother said who is the dread nigga upstairs I said I dont kno but he smoke weed all day. you had to talk to my brother like you was from the streets because he didnt know if you was getting smart or what you were talking about when you were coservative. so he said go ask dude can he sell you a bag foe ten dollars I said I dont know if he sell it but ill ask him so I went up and he sold me a bag for ten. my brother was cool he enjoyed the rest of his night, now I didnt wake up till around nine am they were already woke I fed my baby and played with him he went back to sleep for a nap so I shut my room door and entered the living room goodmorning every one said, I sat down an smoked a cigarette, my brother said go upstairs for me I said naw I already went yesterday, so his lil girlfriend said ill go up there so I opened the door and showed her wut door to go to but all the door were open except one door cause every body else was family so they ran back and forth. she proceeded up the stairs and stopped in front of the door I was at the bottom watching now my brothers girlfriend was very short and she looked young, it was one of the guys eighteenth birthday and it was smokey in the hall they had the music going and they wer standing out with cups they had drinks, she said excuse me is the man of the house here the dread dude came forward and said thats me, she said hi im Tip sister can I buy a bag. Now she should have said im Tip's brother's girlfriend, so by her saying she was my sister and looking young the birthday boy said what tell Tip she sent the right sister, my brother had got up to see what was taking so long and he heard they guy flirting with his girlfriend so he ran pass me and approached the guy he ran in the house and closed the door so the dread dude had his door still standing open, my brother said where did that hoe ass nigga go, dread said who my brother said that hoe ass nigga in the checker shirt, oh dude aint in here so my brother done got heated cause dread pointed next door and said he lives over there, so my brother knocked and lil dude Daddy came to the door he was a big guy my brother said wher that hoe ass nigga at, big dude said who my son my brother said him right there as dude walked out but stayed behind his daddy, his daddy said what he do my brother said he out here trying to talk to my girl and I dont like it, big dude pulled one side of his shirt up and said thats my son my brother said I dont give a fuck hoe ass nigga ill box both of yall, he ran down stairs in my house came back with two nine milimeter guns and pointed at the daddy and the son he what you wanns do hoe ass nigga ill blow this whole building up, the daddy closed his door he was intimidated and the whole time im trying to calm my brother down. he went back to dread door like if you go sell weed sell it and quit bullshitting, dread dude just shook his head. I finally got my brother down the stairs towards my house somebody yelled you better get him out yo house because ima call the police if you dont, my brother yelled fuck the police and if they come ima really knock out a mutha fucka, or have some body come do it. so inside my house im trying calm my brother down I said where did them guns come from I asked him to take them outside by the dumpster somewhere so if they call the police I wouldnt loose my house or my kids. he turned and look at me and said bitch put your baby by the dumpster. I said what nigga yall gotta go he grabbed a glass off the table and drew it back he said say something else and ill buss you upside yo dam head. I said and if you do you will be under the jail. he pulled out one of the guns from his pocket and put it to my head and said bitch ill blow yo head off. I said go head maybe I need to die but I promise you if I get up you will not ever pull a gun out on nobody else he mugged my head to the side with the gun I thought I was dead. I was already depressed and nervious about everything this made it worse, he put the gun back in his pocket and said you know what bitch where im from somebody would have been stabbed you cause you talk to much shit. I never said nothing to him other then help me keep my apartment and kids, I thank god he allowed me to make it by baby was still asleep, and my brother was packing his stuff and left I made a promise to myself that I will never say two more words to him, he can never be welcomed in my home or around my kids, and I hadnt seen him for a couple months after this and my mom called me and said yo brother wanna know if his nephews can come stay the weekend with him, "NO" without letting her explain her self, she said he still your brother. naw he your son I said im done with him. and one week later me and mom went to see wut the free place was giving out and walked pass my brother standing in front of the building he was trying to get away frm my mom, as she stopped and talked to him, He yelled ma get her ass away from here he didnt even let her hug him so we walked off about a block he yelled for my mom to come back and I stopped a stood waitin for her, he hugged her and gave her twenty dollars, like he was making me mad, he called me five days later trying to say he was sorry and asked me if I had money so he can treat his girlfriend it was her birthday. "NO I said as I hung up. I hadn't heard from him since, but I do know that for a while my mom's drug habbit was out of control for a while, expecially when I first hit pubity. she thought she could get everything from the free church. my grandmother had to come down a couple times to make sure we had gotten what we needed she would even keep the receipts so mom couldnt take things back to the store. and to this day me and my mom still goes to the free church. it has always been a dream I had since I was a child to have my children to belong to the same man that I would marry, we would get a house and a dog and just be happy but unfortunately it didnt work out that way for me, I know women that would kill to interact with their boyfriend/man or significant other's mother but not me I couldn't stand my mother in law. I thought this woman was the devil in woman form, me and my children's father has gotten into many altercations over his mother being in our buisness to much he would run to her for everything. and he would get defensive when I said bad things about her we have been married for thirteen years today, and this man has never defended me in no situation when it came to his mother or noone else. we had our days of being together and it wasnt always bad, but majority of the times we couldn't stand each other. I remember during our first three months we were inseperable if you seen one of us you seen the other we was together everyday. I used to love walking pass his hang out spot with my sister ill get all cute and we would walk pass just so I could see him and I would ask her as I pretended not to be looking his way I would ask is he looking she would say yes and here he comes. ill look back and he was coming so I would stop and we would talk about him coming to visit. we talked on the phone all day everyday. and one day we moved in with each other and we began arguing and he would fight me thinking I was cheating on him, I never cheated on him and although he didnt believe it he started acussing me of messing with every body. I remember him picking me up and slamming me on the floor and I was so sick I didnt know wut was wrong with me my back hurted so bad after that, a couple days later I went to the doctor and they told me I was pregnant, nine weeks pregnant to be exact. he apologized over and over again saying im sorry ill never hit you again, when I was about fourteen weeks pregnat he choked me till I couldnt breath, he said the reason for choking me was because I was walking pass nigga's like I was trying to be fast or wanting someone to touch me, and these guys lived out there some stayed in the same complex as me. I guess he felt like I wasnt interested in him anymore because he was messing with a couple people from the neighborhood before me and they all lived close and everytime I said something to him he got mad at me. eventually we stopped talking for a long time until my daughter was born, because I couldnt deal with the abuse anymore. when I was about six months pregnant he told his mother and father that I wasnt pregnant by him, and that he aint know if I was carrying his baby. he started talking to other girl that all of a sudden started saying she had a daughter by him that was three years old. I heard after stories but because she hadn't done anything to me so I wont write about her. lol. I used to have to walk pass them all the time to get to my house because he attended a church close to my home with his family, now his father on the other hand is a beautiful man and I loved him because he was the only one making sure I was ok. his mother used to laugh at me I was big and pegnant she would roll her eyes and talk bad about me, she told me one day my son said that aint even his baby, ok I said, so after my baby was born I went and got a blood test and the automatically put him on child support, he was mad about the child support but had you not denied my daughter you wouldnt had to be. I called to let the family see my daughter they were happy and his mother loved her I dont know if she was pretending because she didnt like me and I never done anything to her, oh how I loved that man and still love him today. his father always snuck and gave me money and said make sure I buy the baby something he said he believed it was his grandchild the whole time. he always lets me know wut a wonderful job I was doing and how good of a mother I am, he would always tell me to keep up the good work. he let me know that if there was anything he could do to help me with the kids just let him know he said dont continue to let the devil win. I remember being asked why did I have so many children and all I could say was because I dont believe in abortions, I have been pregnant eight times thoughout my life. my first time being pregnant it turned out to be an ectopic pregnancy, I believe god does everything for a reason. and I know he wouldnt give me more then I could bare. my husband was once a good guy he didnt believe in doing drugs or illegal activity, he didnt wear his paints hanging off his bottom, and he was so handsome he knew how to satisfy me thats why I fell in love with him, we have seperated and have been seperated for three years, during the begining of our relationship I was pregnant before I had gotten with him and I didnt know, all I knew was I was in so much pain and that I was bleeding really heavy I walked bent over I went to the clinic and they told me that I was having a miscarrage and that I should go home and let it finish passing, they told me to elevate my feet, so I went home and tried to lay down but it was so painful, I couldnt sleep I couldnt elevate my feet and I couldnt stand up straight. I went to the hospital because I was bleeding so heavy I was bleeding through 4 pads within an hour, when I gotten to the hospital they saw I was in so much pain and crying that they rushed me to the back, the doctor took me to the ultra sound room and told me that I was having an ectopic pregnancy, he drew up a diagram of the womens tubes and showed me how my tube was splitting he said that poisonious blood was leaking behind my uteris from my tubes, and that it had formed a blood clot the size of a plum, that is what was causing me to hurt so bad, I was scared because then he said they needed to do surgery I was twenty-one years old. my husband was there every step of the way and I fell deep in love with him he was there from the time I closed my eyes and when I opened my eyes I was so druggy, when I woke up he held my hand and told me he loved me he said that I kept asking for him and reaching back when they was taking me to the surgery room, the doctors came in and asked me how I felt they explained that they didnt have to remove my tubes or cut any out they said they only had to flush it, he also informed me that if I was to get pregnant again that I would continue to have tubals or I would miscarry them from scar tissue on my tubes. So I was discharged and sent home, Where I was invited to stay at my inlaws house for the night, So that I would have help getting around, And I was so grateful a couple months later I prayed that god would bless me with a daughter and that she would be healthy and beautiful, and the begining of the year I got pregnant with my daughter she weighed a healthy 7lbs and 14ozs and two years later I gave birth to my first born son he weighed a healthy 8lbs and 8ozs and the blessings didnt stop there the same yr my son was born I gave birth to a healthy baby girl weighing 7lbs and 5ozs thentwo years later another son was born he weighed 8lbs and 10ozs / during the birth of my fourth son I was so happy I had love finally I knew some one would need me and love me for the rest of my life, when my fourth son turned three months old he came down with a really high fever that I couldnt break, I tried everything to break this fever and I couldnt so I rushed him to cincinnati childrens hospital. they told me that my son had contracted bacterial meningitus on the brain and the spin, they said because of the exema on his jaws that some kind of bacteria had gotten into his pores and it caused him to get sick. the house we lived in had started growing mold up the walls on the side of the furniture and I was young and didnt know much but it was later detected that that was the problem, the doctors explained all the risks of death and other posiblities that could go wrong. I cried like a baby when they said they had to admit him, he was in the hospital for a total of six ina half months before the doctors came in to talk to me they said my son was dead and that they aint know if the medicines they was giving him was working they didnt see enough improvements or sighns that he was getting better they told me my son was basically dead and that I needed to call and make arrangements for people to come see him, oh I was so hurt I cried and cried then finally I looked at my son laying there I have been here for six ina half months with this baby and im not leaving without him. my son had tubes everywhere they was in his sides draining poison off his chest and lungs there were tubes draining poison off his brain, he had a pic line central and all kinds of things his penis had swollen up he had a cathitor, and about eight differant IV's running my son didnt look like himself. I got down on my knees and said father please forgive me, I said father I know your here I can feel your presence if your going to take my son then please take him now dont let him suffer father please because im suffering amen. I got up and kissed my son on the forehead and sat in the chair, I went to sleep because my head was hurting me so bad from crying, it was about 11;45pm I woke up it was 7 am I heard commotion, as I opened my eyes I seen about fourty doctors I rushed over cause I thought my son had passed away. Calling his name I finally got through my son was sitting up on the bed looking around the room, his eyes were barely opened and I hugged him I said baby can you hear me. tears just fell from his eyes he couldnt talk or cry because of the tubes in his throat. he was letting me know he heard me. one doctor shoved me and said move and let us do our jobs, I read that women her rights I been there six long months and my son laid here and couldnt do much and now he woke you move and let my god do his job. she addressed me as mam the remainder of the stay and one week later my son went home Hallelujah thank you jesus for my testimony! my fifth son came the next year he weighed 9lbs and 7ozs and my sixth son came weighing 9lbs and 2ozs finally my last son came weighing 5lbs and 14ozs. the seventh baby was born with downs syndrome, he was born with an incomplete asvd meening the middle of his heart wasnt developed at birth he had so many problems failure to thrive and poor development and growth and some type of allergy to formuls so he had to drink a special milk that was completly broken down and so expensive it was called alimentum is stinks really bad. my son finally had his heart surgery when he was eight months old because the doctors had to wait until his tissue thickened up because they said it would have been like sewing threw snot/water it wouldnt hold so I had to bring him in and out the hospital to be amitted for getting sick, im blessed to have this baby be a part of my life. God said he blessed with with this baby because he got tired of me having a broken heart he sent me someone that would always need me and some one that I would always need, I never tried street drugs I never had a threesome I never popped extasy, I dont go out to bars/clubs and I never even donated blood, how did my son become sick the docters told me that at the time of conception the father and my dna gene wasnt compatable the father was younger and the chromosomes didnt seperate evenly so he had an extra chromosome on one side, I cried during pregnacy but when I seen his face I knew everything would be okay he had ten fingers and ten toes and that was enough for me. I had my children altogether and thats all that mattered, and I wont allow them to go near no one that has hurt me in the past other then my mother I Didn't understand life growing up and what you had to do being a mother, how you had to pay the Bill's and kept up with differant sizes as each child grew up, I enjoyed being a full time mother and I know my children enjoy having me as there mother they fight amungst each other they play amungst each other everyday and I wouldnt have it no other way, I think sitting back watching my kids really gave me insight on what my mom had to go through as a women/ mother and I know now that it was a full time Job, im a single parent seven small children, and I would dare put as much pressure on them they I had. I would never hurt my children because they are part of me. I want women to know that there is light at the end of the tunnel, there is help at the end of the day. abuse comes in many many forms and verbal abuse is just as bad as physical abuse stop it, dont let no one hurt your children because they are a part of you they need you to stand up and fight for them because if you dont who will teach them right from wrong so they wont grow up to be abused or abuse someone else, I wanna say thank you to everybody that helped me along the way and that wanted to help but couldnt . . . I had to learn to rebuild myself after being torn apart for so long it hurted for a while but I made it, when you learn how to forgive it gives you power it gives you control. when your hurting and beat down its up to you to get up, you hold your own future in your hands, you have to decide when enough is enough. and when you get up stay up Love helps you heal not hate, I forgave everyone that hurt me. if you stay with a person that dont appreciate you it will stop you from blossoming, and although I will never forget wut has happened to me throughout my life, I will not let it make me vaunerable to live life for my kids. I thank god for all the trials and tribulations because it was my learning experiance. Today I will not hurt not more. I have eliminated all negative waves I will always believe in god because the devil whispers disbelief and have you thinking you cant win, for someone who hasnt seen such phenomena happen before, Iam proof I am a living testimony, I am free today and I thank you readers with all my heart because someone finally listened . . . YOU listened, I have told so many people that my space was being violated for so many years and no one listened to me, and I reached out and YOU listened, thank you.

SHOUT OUT'S to God my creator, my reader's, my mom for birthing me, my children for inspiring me everyday and telling that I could do it my 13 beautiful neice's for telling me im their favorite aunty. and my 7 nephews for helping me with my featured picture. my sisters, and brothers I love all of yall my aunts and uncles, my friends, I also wanna thank the person that stayed true to herself through all thing's "ME"